Home at Summer's End

BOOKS BY ALYS MURRAY

The Magnolia Sisters
Sweet Pea Summer
The Perfect Hideaway

ALYS MURRAY

Home at Summer's End

Bookouture

Published by Bookouture in 2020

An imprint of Storyfire Ltd.
Carmelite House
50 Victoria Embankment
London EC4Y 0DZ

www.bookouture.com

ISBN: 978-1-80019-053-5
eBook ISBN: 978-1-80019-052-8

To Bubba and Kristina,
For all of the hours we spent watching (and rewatching) the Katy Perry episode of Catfish.

Chapter One

Rose

Rose never minded being the only person in her family unattached. Well, of course, that depended on what you meant by unattached. She may not have had a husband like her mother or her younger sister, Harper, and she may not have had a boyfriend like her youngest sister, May, or her friend, Annie, but she did have a steady relationship with the flower shop she owned and a second one with the historical romance novels she compulsively borrowed from the library.

And, she supposed, it also depended on your definition of "minded". Did she resent her *entire* family and her only friend for pairing off and finding the loves of their lives? No, obviously not. She couldn't ever begrudge someone finding their happiness. But did she get lonely? Yeah. Did she sometimes look out at the long, dirt road leading away from her hometown of Hillsboro, California, and wonder if some strong, sturdy, stalwart, strapping, handsome guy would wander into town and fall madly, desperately, truly, overwhelmingly, riotously in love with her?

Yes, obviously.

Did she also wonder if her habit of mainlining romance novels was infecting, if not her heart, then definitely her vocabulary? Yep. No doubt.

But the thing was, whenever she was lucky enough to have her entire family around, she didn't think about her ever-purpling vocabulary or the way she sometimes felt sick when she caught one of her sisters getting a forehead kiss from the man she loved. No, she was just happy to have them around again. Especially on nights like tonight.

The fall evening hung cool and crisp all around the Anderson Flower Farm, where the Anderson sisters—Rose, Harper, and May—and their best friend, Annie, were currently stationed out on the great porch overlooking the fields of flowers below. With the weather snapping into more and more frequent chill spells the stronger flowers nearby were only just now beginning to bloom and in the light of the stars and the warm glow of the porch, Rose could spot a large patch of callas in the distance, their long, white petals stretching out to dance in the moon-soaked breeze.

With the men of the family inside, caught up in the extra innings of a World Series baseball game, and her mother finishing tidying the kitchen, Rose felt free to finally relax with some of the people she loved most in this world. The men were alright, of course, especially her father, but still…Her family had always been a family of women. Of sisters. Here, with them again, she felt most comfortable.

"So, birthday girl," Annie asked, her blonde curls bouncing as she took another dainty bite of the birthday pie they'd gotten Rose for the occasion, "what did you wish for?"

At least, she felt most comfortable with them when they weren't asking questions like *that*. Suddenly, the attention of the three women settled upon her shoulders. The slice of "Birthday Blueberry Pie" from Millie's Pie Joint stuck in her throat. She tried her best to swallow it before answering.

"You know if I told you, it wouldn't come true."

"Right. Of course. Always the superstitious type."

Rose guessed she was a little superstitious, though she knew it wasn't the label the folks from town usually called her. The "Andersons Plus Annie" foursome was slightly infamous, which meant everyone in Hillsboro had put them directly into boxes. Harper, tall and solid, and operator of the family flower farm, was the badass tomboy. May, who'd recently run off with her ex-boyfriend to travel the world, was the wild child. Annie was the perfect social media starlet. As for Rose, she was the "sweet" one.

No, no one had ever called her superstitious before, but she supposed she was. She believed in birthday wishes. She had always pinned her hopes on falling stars and dandelions. She was never comfortable with walking under a ladder.

Unable to help herself, Rose smiled triumphantly. "I wished for a pony on my seventh birthday pie, told Harper about it immediately, and guess who still doesn't have a pony? It's not superstition; it's just facts. If you tell your wish, it doesn't come true."

"Mom and Dad weren't ever going to get you a pony," Harper snarked, waving her blueberry-stained fork in Rose's direction.

"Not after I blew it with my birthday wish they weren't."

Annie shifted in her seat, clearly wanting to get back to the point. "This isn't about the pony. This is just about you."

"Yes, of course," Rose said, obligingly. "And me not wanting to waste my wish on you three."

This was how it was when they got together. May, Annie, and Harper were excitable and snappy, the kind of women who always had a quip waiting at the tip of their tongue. Rose was used to her role as peacekeeper, as the calm, untouchable eye in the center of their constant storms.

"Fine. You don't have to tell us your wish. Just tell us what you want out of this year. You have three hundred and sixty-four days left to be twenty-eight. What are you going to do with them?"

Rose shrugged. She could tell where Annie was going with this, and it wasn't anywhere she wanted to tag along. Evading the persistent blonde's questions wouldn't last forever, but she figured she could delay the inevitable as long as possible. "Oh, you know. Run a flower shop. Make some perfume. Hopefully eat a lot more pie than I did last year."

"I don't think it's humanly possible for someone to eat any more pie than you do already," Harper intoned.

Rose tossed her head, sending her fiery red braid over her shoulder. "Only one way to find out."

Annie, of course, wasn't satisfied by that answer.

"So, you want to do the same things you've always done, with the exception of possibly becoming a pie-eating champion."

"I like my life," Rose replied, her mouth still half-full of her last bite of pie. "Sorry if that bothers you."

That could have been the end of it. Maybe Annie would have, uncharacteristically, given up and not followed her usual one-track mind. Rose would have taken that over any birthday gift in the world. Instead, May, her youngest sister—*traitor*—just had to speak up. Her voice was low, barely audible over the scraping of forks against their plates, but still…they all heard her.

"Well, you like *most* of your life."

"What's that supposed to mean?" Rose asked, shifting in her chair to get a better look at May, who sat in the chair farthest from hers.

"That came out wrong."

"I hope so!"

But any hope that Rose might have had disappeared when Annie, May, and Harper all shared meaningful, uncertain looks with each other. Oh, no. She recognized that look. She recognized that look because it was the same one she put on before she gave advice to one of the other three. It was a look that said, *We've talked this over; no going back now.* Rose hated that look.

Annie spoke first, setting her pie aside on the wide arm of her deck chair. "We're just—"

"We don't want you to be alone, you know."

Harper hadn't ever been one to pull her punches and Rose couldn't help but reel back as if she'd *actually* been punched. She expected this kind of talk from Annie, who thought herself Northern California's premier matchmaker. She expected it from her boy-crazy mother, who hadn't stopped trying to force her into finding true love since the day she turned fourteen. But she hadn't expected it from Harper and May, who'd practically been dragged kicking and screaming into their own happily ever afters. Blinking blindly, she tried to wrap her head around this new information.

"Oh my God. It's true what they say. All women turn into their mothers."

"We aren't trying to be like Mom. We're just saying—"

"We know you want to fall in love," Harper said. "You've always wanted it."

"And maybe," Annie agreed, nudging Rose's arm conspiratorially, "this is your year."

"I can't believe this is how I'm spending my birthday. What happened to cards and flowers and presents and pie?"

Yes. Fine. It was true. Anyone who knew Rose knew that she had always wanted to find love. She was the romantic type, a hardcore believer in love and fairy tales and the magic of first kisses. Just because it hadn't happened to her yet didn't mean it wouldn't. She wasn't going to rush it and she definitely wasn't going to chase it.

At least, that's what she told herself. And so far it had been a pretty convincing fiction.

May's eyes glinted in the evening light, brimming with so much love that Rose's heart almost cracked in two. "We just think that you were such a big part of our love stories. Maybe it's time you go out and find one of your own."

Nope. This wasn't a conversation that they were going to have. She didn't want her sisters and her best friend worrying over her. "Well. Thanks, guys. But as exciting as my love life is, are there any other topics of conversation we can mine? Maybe the weather, or how my latest dental surgery went?"

Harper protested, but the end of that protest died off before she could finish it. "Rose—"

For a moment, Rose let herself survey the three women before her. She loved them all so deeply, had been there at their sides and rooted for them as they'd fought for their dreams and their love stories. She knew what it was like to want someone to have the happiness that they so clearly deserved.

But this time *they* were looking at *her* with the sad, wanting eyes. And she realized just how uncomfortable that spotlight could be, even if it did come from a good and sincere place.

"I know you're all concerned about me. Believe me, I get that. But, please. Love is going to find me in its own time. I don't need to rush it."

She did her best to indicate an unspoken period, end of discussion at the end of that sentence. Thankfully, it seemed like everyone heard it loud and clear.

"Did you hear they're going to film a movie in Hillsboro?" Rose moved the conversation on.

"I may have heard a thing about it," Annie preened. "And I *may* have been the one to suggest it. The location scout's a friend of mine."

Harper scowled. "Annie, you're going to make this town an L.A. outpost before you're done with us, aren't you?"

"I think our beautiful town deserves to be highlighted in a beautiful movie, don't you?"

"The rents are going to go up," Harper countered. "No doubt about it."

"Not with the rent-control measure that George is championing in his column," Annie returned.

May took a long, deep sip of her sparkling wine before tipping it to the yammering duo in a mockery of a toast. "See, *this* is why Tom and I travel. We never have to worry about small-town politics."

"Ah, you'll come back home one day."

"Not if I can help it. You can't even get decent Pad Thai in this town—"

And that's how it went from there. Thankful that they'd taken the heat off her, Rose allowed herself to sink into the soft corners of the conversation, where she watched as they all bickered back and forth. Here, she was comfortable. She loved sitting back as they teased each other, loved the way that their rapid-fire conversation bounced off of their smiles, loved feeling a part of this fantastic, strange family of friends.

But as their conversation wandered, Rose felt herself drift back to the talk they'd left behind. They all thought she needed romance. And romance would be nice; she wasn't going to deny that. But for Rose, this was enough for right now. To know she loved these people so dearly, and to know that they loved her just as much. Tugging her sweater closer around her, she settled back into her chair, feeling as comfortable wrapped up in the soft, knitted fabric as she did in their chatting.

There was something else, though, too. She was safer in the shadows. Safer as the shy, kind, *nice* Anderson sister. Safer when no one was looking at her, when they all just let her slip through the cracks.

Of course, it couldn't last forever. Eventually, the baseball game inside the house ended, and everyone on the porch was beckoned inside. Rose volunteered to collect the dishes so that her sisters could be reunited with their significant others. She may have loved that they had all found their Person, but that didn't mean she wanted to be stuck in there while they all kissed as if they'd been parted for years instead of just an hour or so.

"…Rose?"

When Annie hung back on the porch for a moment, Rose didn't even have the strength to sigh in exasperation. Annie had always been the most voracious of matchmakers, always trying to set her up with someone or another. After she'd found her own romance with George Barnett, the town's ace newspaper hound, she'd let up a little bit. Still, Rose had been expecting this.

"Mm-hm?" Rose said, not looking up from the pile of plates she was currently assembling.

"Look, I'm not going to make a big thing out of this, but just know…" Annie paused. Rose braced herself for the inevitable. "My offer is still on the table. If you ever want me to help you find someone, someone *not* from this admittedly shallow dating pool… you just have to let me know, okay?"

"Thanks, Annie," Rose said, putting on her bravest face. "But I'm going to be fine."

"I know you are. You're always fine. I just think it would be nice if there was someone to share *fine* with you. Or maybe to even make things great."

Without her permission Rose's eyes darted to the porch window, where she spotted her parents cuddled up on the couch, alongside Tom and May, and Harper and Luke. George hung back, waiting for Annie's return. A pang of jealousy, sharp and clear, stabbed through Rose's chest. She clamped down on the feeling, hard, and smiled her best, most convincing smile for Annie's benefit.

"I'll think about it."

Hours later, the family had dispersed, leaving Rose alone in the kitchen of the big farmhouse where she still lived with her parents—the same farmhouse where, until earlier this year, both of her sisters had lived, too—to wash dishes. Dishes were one of her favorite chores. She loved the ritual of it, the way the world could melt into the soap bubbles and the repetition of washing and drying.

Dishes usually gave her time to think, too. To run through the events of the day and put her thoughts in order. Today, the facts were these. She was twenty-eight years old. She had never been in love—no time that had counted anyway. And despite the fact that she was okay with that, no one else seemed to be.

Well. Fine. They didn't have to be okay with it. Or with her methods of patiently waiting for the right person to come along. They only had to accept it.

Unfortunately, there was one person who wouldn't ever accept it. Somewhere, in the middle of her dishwashing ritual, she found a pair of hands squeezing her shoulders and a warbling, sickly sweet voice piping up behind her.

Her mother. Her mother, who was here to once again bemoan the fact that Rose—her favorite daughter, the daughter she'd always called the most beautiful, the most agreeable, the most marriageable—was still single, long after everyone else had found their Person.

"Oh, dear. How are you holding up?"

"I'm fine, Mom. I'm just going to miss them, that's all."

That seemed like a good enough excuse. May and Tom were off on their next adventure, a quick trip between tonight's birthday celebration and their engagement party in two weeks. Better to focus on that than what her mother was, no doubt, *really* worried about.

"Rose Anderson. You don't have to lie to me. I know what's really going on here."

The smile she plastered on her face almost hurt now. "And what is that?"

Her mother moved around the counter, so she could face her, piercing her with the full weight of her pitying gaze. "You're feeling the same way I would in your position. You want what they have, don't you? Don't worry. You'll find it someday, my girl. I promise. Someday, some fantastic man is going to open his eyes and see what a gem my first daughter is. So, don't you worry, okay?"

"I'm not worried—"

"Hush. Don't say another word. Your secret is safe with me."

With one more gentle touch on her shoulder, her mother floated out of the room, humming Mendelssohn as she went. Rose clenched the plate in her hand so hard she almost broke it. *Why* did everyone think she was some breakable, sad thing just because she didn't have a man in her life? Why did they all look at her like she was going to shatter any second, like her life had no meaning and no joy just because she wasn't dating someone?

A fire ripped through her, scalding any last remnants of her old way of thinking. Yes, of course they cared about her and, yes, of course they wanted her to be happy. But that didn't give any of them—not her sisters, not her mother, not *anyone*—the right to treat her this way.

Before she could think better of it, Rose dropped her plate in the soapy water, wiped her hands on her jeans, and hit the most recent contact in her phone's dial history. After two rings, a warm, honeyed voice chirped on the other end of the line.

"Hello?"

"Annie?"

"Rose, what's up?"

For a brief second, Rose almost lost her nerve. Just like she lost her nerve about everything. About her dreams of making perfume. About falling in love. About taking most risks in her life. But it only took one thought of her mother's whining, sickly-sweet tone to make up her mind. Not only was it the right thing to do. It was the *only* thing to do. If she couldn't buck up the courage to follow her dreams, the least she could do was get her mother off her back about her premature spinsterhood. Instinctively, she gripped the phone tighter.

"Did you mean what you said? About setting me up with one of your friends?"

In her mind's eye, she could envision her friend perking up, positively gleeful at the thought.

"Are you *serious* right now? It's all I've ever wanted. Of course I meant it."

Rose drank in a deep breath, centering herself. A small, secret smile tugged at her lips.

"Okay. Because I think I'm ready."

Chapter Two

Cole

There was more to Cole McKittrick than his rippling abs. And his square jawline that could cut through glass or a woman's heart. And his deep, American voice that made everything he said sound like the bold text in a *Superman* comic. And his winning smile, warm and honest enough to make strangers swoon and would-be enemies crumble.

That's what he'd come here, to the provincial hamlet of Hillsboro, California, to prove. That there was more to him than met the eye. When he was just twenty-one, he'd been plucked out of obscurity to play the heartthrob, bad-boy coming of age son in a too-long running television show—the kind of guy who they showed shirtless in the opening credits. Now, eight years later, with the contract renewal for *Crime Spree: Beach City* gathering dust in the depths of the "trash" folder on his agent's computer, he was finally ready for something bigger. Something more.

Oh, and he was ready to eat cheeseburgers again. *So* ready to eat cheeseburgers.

That was the other great thing about doing a movie where there was more to your character than how he looked when he took off his shirt. You could afford to live a little in the dining department of your life.

Retreating to Hillsboro from Los Angeles wouldn't have been his first choice to launch his post-*Crime Spree: Beach City* life, but at least he would have plenty of opportunities to gorge himself on small town diner food.

As he browsed the shelves of a bookstore—Talley's, it was called—his stomach growled, but not so loud that he couldn't hear the sound of a slightly shrill voice announce itself behind him.

"I'm so sorry, are you Cole McKittrick?"

The problem with filming a movie in the cutest small town in America? He stood out like a sore thumb. It seemed here that everybody knew everyone in Hillsboro, which meant that any unfamiliar faces got extra scrutiny. And when people found that they recognized him not from the pews of their local church or the pages of their high school yearbook but from television, well, they either pointedly ignored him and tried to give him privacy, which made him feel even *more* out of place. Or, they were like this. Stopping behind him in the twee, cat-filled bookstore on the town's main square to try and get his attention.

Seeing no point in pulling his cap down lower over his forehead, Cole forced a smile to his lips and tried to hide the stack of romance novels under his arm as he turned to face the stranger. "You've got a good eye. Please, call me—"

The words died in his throat as he finally came face to face with her. Not a fan. But Annie Martin. A familiar face in this small-town sea of strangers. Relief washed over him, and he couldn't help but smile. Annie had always been a Hollywood wild card, especially after she and her brother both abandoned Los Angeles and decamped to Hillsboro, but ever since he'd met her a few years ago at an industry party, they'd been friendly. She'd even been the one to suggest the film shoot here.

The blonde, who always managed to look like she'd stepped out of her own perfect Instagram feed, burst into laughter.

"Gotcha!"

"What did you do that for?" Cole said, the smile not leaving his face even as his heart rate slowed to a more reasonable tempo. "I thought I was about to face down a horde of ravenous fans."

Annie's smile was innocent, but it quickly turned sour as she spoke. "I wanted to make sure that you weren't going to go totally Hollywood on the people of this town. Trust me. Some of your co-stars that I've run into have not passed the test so well."

"Oh, yeah?" he prompted.

Sensing that he wasn't going to get rid of Annie any time soon, Cole turned to continue surveying the bookstore shelves all around him. Plenty of people warned him about how much he would miss big-city culture once he started small-town movie living, but so far he hadn't quite caught that bug. Sure, he missed 24-hour smoothie deliveries and a steady stream of Ubers, but mostly he found himself charmed by the rustic, western-style architecture of Hillsboro and the people. And despite the fact that books hadn't really been his thing until last week—he'd always been more of a binge-watching TV type—part of him didn't want to leave the cozy warmth of this bookshop, with its sweet, snoozing fat cats curled up on various bookshelves, and the collection of titles, which he could somehow tell had been chosen with great care and love.

"Yeah. Let's just say Fiona Marks isn't as friendly as she seems on TV."

"I heard that rumor, actually."

More than rumor, he'd experienced Fiona Marks's prickly personality firsthand during rehearsals for this film. It was part of the reason he was here, actually. In the film he was about to shoot Cole would play a young, hotshot lawyer forced to team up with a small-town lawyer to defend an innocent man accused of murder. Over the course of that struggle he would, of course, fall in love with his fellow lawyer's young daughter and learn the true meaning of justice, love, community…blah, blah, blah.

The movie would hinge on his chemistry with his co-stars. So far he hadn't had any trouble with Andrew Wagner, the esteemed, but slightly washed-up actor playing the older lawyer. With Fiona, though? It was like talking to a brick wall.

Hence, the romance novels. Despite Fiona's rough exterior and impersonal demeanor, Cole wasn't just going to give up and blame it all on her. If he wanted this movie to work—this movie that was going to save his career after he quit a dead-end TV show and lost his tabloid-fodder girlfriend—then he needed to put in the effort, too. And that started with a little bit of research in the romance section.

Sure, he could rewrite a few lines in the script here and there. Do his best to make audiences fall in love with the character who'd gone through so many rewrites and screenwriters and script doctors that Cole didn't even know who he was anymore. But all of that started with research.

The suggestion had been made by his director's secretary, who'd loaned him his first well-worn romance paperback, and now he wanted to gobble up as many of these things as possible. Not *just* for work, either.

There were some personal reasons too.

"It's a shame," Annie tutted, picking up and then putting down a few books of her own. "Because you and Fiona Marks look really cute together. I can already see the movie poster."

Before he could stop himself, Cole grumbled, "There needs to be a movie before there's a movie poster, you know?"

It was the wrong thing to say. He should have remembered that Annie never let anything slip past her, especially not where gossip was concerned. He tried to play it cool as she raised one plucked eyebrow in his direction.

"And are you foreseeing trouble on that front?"

"Why would you say that?"

"Besides the fact that you look like someone ate all of the donuts at the Craft services table?"

Truth be told, Cole's stomach grumbled ravenously at the mere mention of donuts. He couldn't remember the last time he'd had one of those. He made a mental note to find the town's best bakery and get lost there.

He shrugged. "Sure. Besides that."

"It could be the stack of romance novels you're trying to hide under your coat. Doing a little bit of research, are we?"

"Oh, these?" He cleared his throat, eyes dashing around out of habit. No one in this corner of the shop to overhear them but the cats. Still, he tried to cover, not wanting to show even a hint of weakness. "No, this is my usual genre of reading."

"Really? Because last time I went to your place in The Hills I don't remember seeing a magazine, much less a book, anywhere."

Caught again. Annie Martin was good. As excited as he had been to film a movie in a town where he knew someone, suddenly he was wondering if being friends with her was such a good idea. He wasn't used to having people around who saw straight through him.

Cole lowered his tone. "I played an unattainable badass on TV for seven seasons. I just want to make sure I'm not going to screw up my first big movie after that, you know?"

"I think you're going to be *great*. You're always great."

"Yeah, great at playing the same character for years on end."

Annie paused for a moment, clearly trying to scrape together some kind of compliment to salvage the situation. While he waited, Cole picked up two more paperbacks and added them to his stack. Finally, Annie snapped her fingers excitedly.

"You were in that other movie. That one about saving that girl from a kidnapper. That was pretty good."

He had to swallow back a laugh. That piece of garbage had almost ruined his career. "Yeah, so good that they pulled it from theaters and buried it on a streaming service, like, two weeks after it opened."

"Streaming's where it's at anyway," Annie said, with a shrug. "I usually get kicked out of movie theaters when I try to act there the way I do at home."

Not knowing quite what to say to that little joke, for a moment, Cole focused his energies on the books in front of him. Books with soft, sweeping covers and eyes filled with longing. He'd wanted to challenge himself as an actor. To work with a great director on a great script and show everyone what he could do. He could almost hear his mother's voice in the back of his head. *Be careful what you wish for.*

If this movie went south then everyone would be just like Annie. Well-meaningly reminding him of his failure. He swallowed hard and added another book blindly to his stack. No. He wouldn't let that happen.

"You know, as fantastic as this reunion has been, does it happen to have a point?" he asked, trying not to sound unkind.

"Trying to get rid of me?"

"I'm trying to buy my books and go back to my hotel so I can read them. You know. How bookstores work."

"I told you. I saw you in the window and wanted to make sure that you weren't going to be a jerk to everyone in this town."

Cole's hand paused over the bookshelf he currently perused. Everyone in L.A. talked about how weird it was, Annie retreating out here to the country and joining up with the locals. They whispered about whether or not she'd finally cracked, about whether this was the sign of some kind of breakdown that her brother was trying to hide from the world. Cole didn't see any signs of that. Instead, he saw something else, something possibly more ridiculous. Love. She loved this town and the people in it.

He couldn't imagine loving anything so much.

"You're really protective of them, aren't you?"

"They're good people. They've been very good to me." Dropping her voice, she nudged him conspiratorially, managing to only slightly wince when she hit the solid, toned muscles of his ribcage. "I want to make sure that you guys won't embarrass me in front of my cool friends, alright?"

Cole raised his lips in a smirk. It was nice not to have to pretend in front of Annie. Not to have to put on the handsome, perfect, movie star act he had with everyone else. "I promise. Cross my heart. I won't scare off the locals with my zany, big-city ways. I won't even try to sell them any of that snake oil I've been trying to move."

"Very funny," Annie deadpanned.

"Satisfied?"

The way she looked up at him then, from under her too-long-to-be-natural eyelashes, told him that she most certainly wasn't. Sure enough, she needed no more prodding from him to get right to the point. Annie wasn't ever one to keep things bottled up inside, at least as far as he knew. It was one of the things he liked about her. Many of the women he knew liked to play coy and beat around the bush. The farthest Annie ever went in that direction was her matchmaking schemes, and he was safe from that, thank God.

"No. Actually," Annie said, leaning against a bookshelf to block his path to the checkout counter. She toyed with a pair of oversized, bright purple sunglasses in her hand. "There is one more thing."

"I'm listening."

A dimple appeared in Annie's left cheek as her smile broadened. At the sight of it, Cole's stomach plummeted. "If you really wanted to learn how to be a good romantic hero, I think I know just the girl for you."

No. He'd thought he would be safe from this. From Annie and her delusions of romantic grandeur. Cole was *off* of the market, and these romance novels were part of the reason why.

"Are you *still* trying to set people up?"

"No!" Annie had the gall to look offended by the question. "Absolutely not! This is purely for your research purposes. My friend, Rose Anderson, is the most voracious romance reader I've ever met. She must have a library at home full of those books. I bet she could help you out."

After digging in her purse for a moment, she eventually retrieved a small business card. The bold, typeface letters read ANDERSON FLOWER MARKET with an address and a phone number, but scrawled in Annie's cute, pink, flourishing handwriting was the name Rose Anderson, and a phone number he could only assume was the woman's cell phone number.

"And…?"

"And if the two of you happen to fall wildly in love and become one of those legendary Hollywood romances, then I certainly won't be sad about it," she added, with a wink.

"I think you know I'm not really in the market for a relationship right now, Annie," Cole said, gripping his stack of romance novels until his knuckles went white.

"You know what they say. It always comes when you least expect it."

He tried to be good-natured about this. Annie was, of course, just trying to help. Even if her way of helping was to stab him right through the heart. He tried to work his way past Annie to the checkout counter, where maybe he would get away from this little tête-à-tête. "I'm not *not* expecting it. I'm actively rejecting it. I am putting up all of my do not fall for me signals. Do not fall in love. Do not collect two hundred dollars. Do not—"

"Treat you like Vivienne Matilde did?"

Just her name. That was all it took to wipe the trying smile from Cole's lips and to stop his desperate attempts to flee. He was rooted to the spot. His mouth filled with the taste of battery acid. His heart? Well, for a moment that just stopped working altogether.

Vivienne Matilde had been, at least until a few months ago, the love of his life. The only problem was, it turned out that he wasn't hers. The tabloid press did what they did best, getting exactly every detail of the breakup wrong, but Cole was okay with that. He didn't need anyone knowing the truth.

Because the breakup wasn't going to last. With the help of these romance novels and the lessons they contained, he wasn't just going to crush his first big, post-*Crime Spree* movie role. No. He was going to win back the woman he loved.

"You know," he said, his eyes flickering up to meet Annie's, "the people who work for me don't even say her name."

"Yeah, well, I don't work for you, Cole." Annie peered at the top of his romance novel tower, plucked the top one away, and replaced it with another from a nearby shelf. She gave herself a self-satisfied nod as she continued. "And if I did, I'd make sure that you employ the services of one Rose Anderson to make sure that you're the most suave, brilliant, swoony romantic hero since Cary Grant."

"I was always more of a Jimmy Stewart guy myself."

"I don't believe you've ever seen a black-and-white movie."

She had him there. If it didn't have explosions or a Tom Hanks cameo, it probably wasn't in his usual movie night rotation. He chuckled.

"Not true. I saw *The Wizard of Oz* once," he said, by way of deflecting.

But Annie wasn't satisfied with that. And not because *The Wizard of Oz* was only partly in black and white, either. Not with his good-natured attempt to keep the banter going. Not his dismissal of her little plot to get him to fall in love. When he realized she wasn't going to say anything, his head dropped.

"You're not going to let this go, are you?"

"Nope."

"And you've already set us up, haven't you?"

"Yep. You're meeting her at the Torchbearer Wine Cave at six thirty."

As she turned to leave the shop, Cole resisted the urge to roll his eyes. Annie really did think of everything.

"Golden hour. Very nice. Very romantic."

A few steps away, Annie paused and turned on her heel. She shot him a meaningful look.

"And Cole?"

"Yeah?"

A pause. Annie's pink lipstick flattened into a thin, colorful line as she considered what she was going to say next. With her sunglasses back over her eyes, Cole couldn't quite gauge her expression. "Not all women are Vivienne Matilde. It won't kill you to open up your heart a little bit."

"It's not going to happen, Annie."

It's not going to happen because I will win Vivienne back. No matter what tricks you pull.

"You're an actor. If you can't do it for real, then fake it."

Chapter Three

Rose

The Torchbearer Wine Cave was one of the most romantic spots in all of Hillsboro. Carved into the side of a mountain, the cave inside was part storage center, part tasting room, part gothic daydream, with its vaulted stone ceilings and grand, wrought-iron candle chandeliers occasionally dripping wax onto the floor. Outside, tasters could picnic and adjust their eyes to the sunshine with sweeping views of the entire valley, but Rose preferred the quiet, cool interior.

As Rose sat at her table, waiting for this set-up Annie had made for her, she would have been lying if she said she'd never pictured herself sharing some romantic evening here with a stranger. Sipping wine, laughing, talking about their dreams and telling stories about their pasts, watching the candlelight dance in his eyes and wondering if he wanted to kiss her as much as she wanted to kiss him. Although maybe not so much of the sipping wine, since she was the town's most notorious lightweight. The fantasy was as vivid and real to her as any memory, a piece of her imagination so crisp that she could almost reach out and touch it.

Because no matter what she'd let Annie believe about tonight—it wasn't a date. It was the beginnings of her plan to get her family off of her back.

"Rose," Marilou, the usual hostess, said, coming up to her chosen table with slightly uncertain and almost excited eyes. "There's a man here to see you."

"Oh, yes. That must be my…friend. He's new in town and Annie Martin just wants someone to show him around."

"*Just* a friend?"

Rose tried not to prickle at the implication of that question. Like everyone was so frenzied at even the slight possibility of her seeing someone socially.

"Well, not yet, but—" Leaning out of her chair, Rose inclined her neck so as to better see around the waitress and into the small reception just beyond the tasting room. There wasn't anyone there. "Where is he?"

"Well, you usually come alone, so I didn't want to bring him in here unless I was *sure* he was with you, you know how people are. I left him in the bottle cellar."

"It's okay. You can bring him in."

Once Marilou was gone, Rose practically buried herself in her menu, just so she could mutter to herself in private.

"You can do this. You're going to be alright. It's just a non-date. What could possibly go wrong?"

"You know. I don't think I've ever had a woman give herself a pep talk before going on a date with me. Guess it's true what they say. There really is a first time for everything."

Rose, still bent over the menu, found that breathing suddenly became incredibly difficult. She recognized that voice, smooth and deep and distinctly American, like a parody of a wartime ad from the 1940s. She'd heard it a million times through the walls of the family farmhouse, as Harper and May religiously watched *Crime Spree: Beach City*, the long-running show about cops and their delinquent children that became a nationwide sensation.

Slowly, she raised her eyes off of the menu, and followed the strong, lean lines of tailored fabric up the man's body. In dark-wash denim and a soft, dark-blue sweater, he might have passed for normal if he hadn't had such an ungodly form. He was all muscle, all hard edges and sharp lines. Lines that didn't stop when she reached that eminently photogenic face of his, the face she'd seen in ads for everything from his television show to expensive European perfume.

Rose had always tried to be one of those people who saw beneath a person's exterior first. Looks could be deceiving, after all, and she wanted to really know people, not just skim the surface of them. But even she couldn't deny the way her stomach jumped when her eyes reached Cole McKittrick's face. With his perfectly chiseled jawline, his sweep of jet-black hair and his piercing blue eyes that looked somehow more brilliant in person, he was gorgeous. Even the slight dimple in his chin only added to his perfection.

Weirdly, though, it wasn't the angelic look of him that got her. It was the fact that he was Cole McKittrick, famous guy, that sent her heart plummeting to the floor.

She'd come here with a plan. And if this was the "really sweet, super down-to-earth" guy that Annie had thought to set her up with, then it was all ruined. A movie star wasn't ever going to agree to what she'd been scheming.

Before she could stop herself, her voice dropped and she muttered, "Oh, you've got to be kidding me."

A husky, warm laugh washed over her, sending goosebumps down the back of her neck. Oh, yeah. This guy was definitely bad news. His arrogant smirk deepened the dimple in his chin.

"And apparently I'm disappointing, too. I'm really batting zero today, aren't I?"

Rose slammed her eyes shut. This couldn't be happening. Annie had done a lot of ridiculous things over the course of their friendship, but there was no way she would have sent a celebrity to come on this date with her. She'd assumed that it would be some money man from Los Angeles, or maybe a nice, gentle guy who'd come into town to work on the movie. But Cole McKittrick? No. Couldn't be. Rose brought her hands to her temples and started rubbing.

"It can't be you. This is a bad dream. I'll wake up in my bed with a half-drunk glass of hard cider and my cat in my lap and this will all have been a bad dream."

This time, the chuckle wasn't arrogant. It was almost self-conscious. "With all due respect, miss, you aren't doing much for a guy's confidence over here. The, uh, waitress is staring, though, so if you don't mind I'm going to sit down. Can I buy you a drink?"

He didn't wait for an answer before taking the chair across from her. Under the table, Rose surreptitiously pinched her hand. And then, when the wine cave around her didn't disappear into darkness and the man in front of her seated himself opposite her, Rose slunk back in her chair. Bitter embarrassment and disappointment commingled in her mouth, making her want to run out of the room and throw up.

Not quite what she'd expected to be feeling on a date with a celebrity, but she couldn't help it. Cole McKittrick was ruining her plans. And her night.

"So, Annie really did set me up on a date with a movie star."

"TV star, really. But, yes. I'm afraid so."

TV star. He said it so blithely, so easily. Without a hint of modesty.

"Well. My name is—"

"Rose Anderson. You're famous, you know. At least to anyone who knows Annie Martin. And I'm—"

"Cole McKittrick. I'm familiar."

A moment ago, Rose wouldn't have thought it was possible for his chest to get any more puffed out, or for his *I'm a sex god celebrity, so why don't you just bow down already* smirk to get any broader, but in the blink of an eye, he proved her wrong. Stretching back in his chair like he owned the place, he turned the full force of his eyes squarely on her.

"Ah, I see," he said. His gasp reminded her of a detective who'd just been given the final clue to solving a twisted mystery. "Annie set you up because you always had a crush on me, didn't you?"

"No."

Rose didn't have crushes, and she certainly didn't get them on people whose job was essentially to lie for a living. And even if she did have a total lapse in judgment and develop such a crush, the last person she would have confessed that information to would have been Annie. Her protest was barely a glancing blow against his impenetrable armor.

"Oh, yes. I bet your walls were covered with posters of me, right? Slept with a folded-up magazine cut-out of me under your pillow?" He was teasing her, she knew, but she also knew that she wanted to knock the words right out of his mouth. "When you found out I was coming into town, did you beg Annie to make this little meeting happen?"

"No."

"It's okay. You can admit it."

"Wow."

For a long moment, Rose didn't speak, but when she did, that was all she could come up with. *Wow.* Sure, she was familiar with Cole McKittrick's devil-may-care television persona, but in the interviews and late-night shows she'd been forced to watch him on he'd always seemed so nice, so down-to-earth. Apparently, he was a better actor than she'd originally given him credit for. For a moment, she forgot that she had only wanted Annie to set her up on a fake date.

This guy was a jerk. And no matter how she turned it over in her head, she couldn't fathom why Annie had pushed them together. Sure, he was handsome. She could give him that, no problem. But surely Annie knew by now that Rose wasn't the kind of person who could be swayed by a pretty face. When she did one day fall in love she wanted someone with heart and passion, someone with a goodness deep inside that couldn't be denied or hidden away. It was clear that the man sitting across from her didn't possess any of those particular qualities.

"Wow *what?*" Cole volleyed back.

"Annie really does have a talent for seeing the best in people. She talked about how great you were and, with all due respect Mr. McKittrick, I really don't see it."

He narrowed his eyes, slightly. "Likewise."

This was…uncharacteristically bold of Rose, to say the least. Everyone around Hillsboro knew her as the quiet, gentle, agreeable one of the three sisters. The one that everyone could get along with. The one who could see good in everyone and everything.

But if she was being honest, she was getting tired of being the good sister. Where had it gotten her so far? On a date with an absolute jerk, set up by someone she'd thought was one of her best friends.

A smarter version of Rose would have left right then and there. Harper and May and Annie certainly would have. But Rose couldn't help but stand her ground, tossing out one more defense of herself for good measure.

"For what it's worth, not that I think you'll believe me if the size of your wristwatch has anything to do with the size of your ego, but I didn't tune in to your TV show."

"Really? Not a fan of cops and robbers?"

"No, I'm not a fan of bad writing. Or bad production design. Or bad acting."

The second she said all of that she wished she could take it back. Not only was it unkind, but it was untrue. Words spoken in anger and nothing more. From what she had seen of him, he was actually a pretty good actor.

He snapped the menu shut, and all the good acting in the world couldn't hide the fact that all the color had drained from his face. She'd wanted to hurt his feelings and it seemed she'd succeeded.

"You're right. Annie isn't a good judge of character. She said you were the nicest person she's ever met, that you wouldn't hurt a fly. And yet, here you are. Attacking me on a first date."

But before Rose could protest and explain exactly why she wasn't Miss Prim and Proper tonight, Bernard, the owner of the wine cave, wandered over with a small notepad and a familiar smile. If he thought there was anything weird about a celebrity sitting at a table with a customer who usually came here alone, he didn't mention it.

"Rose. It's so good to see you. I don't have to ask you if it's *your* first time here. But you, uh," Bernard said, stumbling over whether to actually call the famous man by his famous name in such a public setting, "sir, is this your first time tasting with us?"

"Yes. But I'm very happy to be here."

A fire lit in Rose's stomach. Where had *this* friendly, warm guy been the last ten minutes? That was actors for you. Professional liars who could turn their charm and emotions on and off at will.

It would have been impressive. It might have made her jealous, too, if it didn't make her blood boil.

"Well, we recommend getting you started out on our four-set, which includes our four best sellers and a little treat to accompany your last glass. I hope you came thirsty though, because we like to pour pretty generously here."

"Oh, you don't have to worry about me, Bernard," he said, his eyes dancing down to the man's name tag, which he wore proudly over his heart. "I'm always thirsty. We'll take the four-set. Thank you so much."

As Bernard slipped away to get them started on their tasting flight, Rose couldn't help but see the man across from her in a new light. Not necessarily a better one, but a new one. He was pretending. Half of him was a lie. She just couldn't tell if it was the half sitting here with her, or if it was the half that had just been so nice to Bernard.

"You're so charming, aren't you?"

Cole shrugged; the casual gesture drew her attention to his shoulders, which were so broad and so strong she longed to reach out and run her hands along them, just to see if they were really as muscular as they looked. "Annie wanted to make sure I don't scare off the locals. I promised her I'd be nice. But back to the point. Where is the sweet, soft Rose Anderson I was promised on this date?"

Rose stiffened. This was the sort of question she always got from people when she didn't act exactly how they wanted her to. The implications of it grated on her.

Also, this wasn't a date. She needed to make that perfectly clear.

"Kindness is not a weakness. I'm not just going to let people walk all over me because I'm nice." She swallowed hard. Tilted her chin. Tried to regain control of this rapidly spiraling evening. "And besides, this isn't a date."

"Oh? That's not what I was told."

"Annie doesn't have all of the facts," she informed him.

"What? Is this an episode of some prank show? Where are the cameras?"

As he playfully scanned the room all around them, Rose watched as he tried to pretend, tried to hide his real emotions. But his smile was uneasy; the emotion didn't meet his eyes. For a brief, glimmering moment, she could see the man behind the mask. As if he *was* really worried that someone would come out and declare this all a joke, an elaborate prank. As if the idea of him being on an actual date was so absurd that, of course, someone would want to take advantage of it for a paparazzi story.

The options were clear. Either Annie purposefully sent Rose on a date with a horrible, arrogant guy who couldn't see past his own nose, or that horrible, arrogant guy was just putting on an act to protect himself. Suddenly, Rose knew which one was happening here. The bravado slithered out of her. Compassion crept into its place.

"I...I'm sorry," she said, her expression softening. "I was wrong."

"Wrong about what?"

"I don't think Annie *is* a bad judge of character. You're just a pretty good actor, aren't you? This," she said, gesturing to just about all of him, "isn't who you really are. I'd bet my life on it."

"What makes you say that?"

The tension between them tightened. Rose leaned forward, lowering her voice. To her surprise, Cole mirrored her actions, until they were both just a candle's distance away from each other.

At first, it had just been a hunch based on one passing expression that faded away at almost the exact same moment she'd caught sight of it. But the more she thought about it, the more sense it made to put her first impression of him aside. She thought through everything she knew about this figure. He'd spent most of his adult life in the public spotlight. He was trying to jumpstart his career all over again after leaving a beloved television show. He'd recently gone through a pretty nasty, pretty publicized breakup...

She was glad now that she hadn't walked out the moment he'd insulted her.

"I've read the magazines. Usually, they're the only thing to read in Annie's house. You're trying to protect yourself, aren't you? From whatever happened—"

He cut her off before she could mention the name of the starlet who'd recently thrown him over.

"I'm just trying to get through this date, alright? So that Annie doesn't set me up on any more."

It ended with a question mark, but she knew that he was trying to end the conversation, *period*. Despite his attempt to shut her down, a light bulb went off in the back of her mind.

"That's a shame."

"Why?"

The wheels in Rose's head were definitely turning now, and they were grinding up her original plan and reforming it into something that could not only help her out, but one that could help the guy sitting across from her, too.

"Because if you weren't a jerk, if you needed some help avoiding Annie, then maybe…Maybe I have a plan that would help us both."

Cole's gaze focused on her again, appraising her as if for the first time. "What kind of plan?"

Chapter Four

Cole

He'd been hoping she would be old. A lovely, old, wise woman who would hand him some romance novels and leave him in peace. Or, barring that, he was hoping she would at least have the decency to not be his type.

He had all the bad luck.

The moment he'd seen Rose Anderson in person, he'd had to fight his natural urge to turn the charm all the way up to eleven. She was the kind of accidental, heart-stopping beauty that you'd never see in Hollywood. So natural she might as well have walked out of the woods or stepped straight out of the ocean. Even sitting down, he could tell she was tall, and the shock of red hair set into a simple braid drew his attention to her easy, gentle features and the long, elegant sweep of her neck and shoulders. The blue cat-eye glasses perched on her nose gave her a bookish, approachable vibe, which somehow made her all the more sexy. *I'd like to check you out of this library, madame librarian.*

Her big, green eyes were far too incisive, though, and as beautiful as she was, she also seemed to be the one person on earth who hadn't bought his act. When Annie had told him that this woman he was going out with was the shy, retiring type, he'd thought that putting on a big show of movie star jerkery would be enough to scare her off. That usually worked when he wanted to get out of something. He should have known that someone like Annie wouldn't have been foolish enough to have friends like that. Of course she'd have friends with plans and thoughts and ambitions of their own.

His question—"What kind of plan?"—hovered in the air as Bernard brought their tasting flights of wine and explained the different varietals. The final wine was accompanied by a dark chocolate, sea-salted peanut butter cup, which Cole wanted to devour immediately, tasting order be damned.

But as soon as Bernard's back was turned, Rose took a tentative, first sip of the first glass of wine, and asked her question as she gazed at him over its rim.

"So, why did Annie send you on this date tonight?"

"She's Annie. Does she even need a reason to go matchmaking?"

"No, she definitely doesn't. But she told me that there was something you needed from me and I can't imagine a guy like you wants for very much. Definitely not dates."

A sarcastic quip bubbled to his lips. *Oh, so you don't think I need any help in the dating department? Why is that? My devilish good looks?* He swallowed it back, though. He wasn't playing that arrogant character anymore. Slowly, he gave himself permission to be normal again.

"It's a professional inquiry. I need some help with research for my role," he said, hedging his bets, not quite wanting to show his cards before she did. The last thing he needed was someone untrustworthy running around town, telling everyone who would listen that the romantic lead in this major motion picture couldn't muster a lick of chemistry with his co-star.

"What kind of research? I'm not really an expert in anything. Unless you need some flower arranging."

From what Cole had heard, that wasn't quite true. Annie insisted that she was a true renaissance woman, running her own business, crafting bouquets and arrangements, and even experimenting with her own line of homemade perfumes. But the question about his research struck too close for comfort, so he flipped the conversation back onto the beautiful woman across from him. It certainly would have been an easier task if her eyes hadn't been so striking, so transfixing. He took another sip of wine, barely tasting it as it slipped down his throat.

"Why did she want *you* to come here?"

"I asked for a date. But, *not* because I really wanted one."

"Interesting. What do you mean by that?"

Who would ask for a date if they didn't want one? Wasn't that the point of going on a date? To be happy with another person? Apparently, Rose Anderson didn't think so. He watched as she squirmed slightly in her seat and fiddled with the stem of the third soldier in her small army of wine glasses.

"I—You promise you won't laugh?"

"Cross my heart."

He was here, on an arranged date he didn't want to come on, with someone who didn't want to be here either. It was the height of comedy, but the joke was on him.

"It's going to sound stupid, but I promise you, what I'm feeling is real."

That straightened Cole's spine. Not just the words, but the way she said it. With a real vulnerability he wouldn't have expected from anyone else in his acquaintance. She was letting him, a veritable stranger, in on a secret. Sure, at conventions and fan meet-ups people had trusted him with stories and truths about themselves— my father passed away and *Crime Spree: Beach City* helped me grieve; I was struggling with my relationship with my brothers, but we became close through watching your show—but while all of those moments had been important to him, this one stood out. Annie had believed that this would last beyond one date; if that was true, then this was a shared secret he'd have to carry with him from here on out. He swallowed as the weight of that responsibility settled down upon his shoulders.

"My entire family is paired off now. My younger sister, Harper, fell in love with Annie's older brother, then my youngest sister fell back in love with her old high school boyfriend and then even Annie fell in love with this newspaper guy from here in town and my parents are two of those people who still sometimes act like they're teenagers in love, so…"

"So, you're the only one who's still alone?"

"I'm not alone," she snapped, her voice and her eyes blazing so hot they nearly scalded him.

But the scalding wasn't painful. It was…weirdly cathartic. After he'd lost Vivienne, everyone treated him differently. Everyone talked about the sad, lonely man he now was, as if he didn't have friends and family and work colleagues who filled up his life. People acted like Vivienne had been his entire world, as if he was nothing and no one without her.

He knew the pain of fighting against that. He knew how Rose Anderson felt. And when he looked into her blazing eyes, for the first time, he didn't see some set-up that Annie had made on his behalf. He saw something like a kindred spirit.

"Sorry. I mean, you're the only one who hasn't found your *soulmate* yet."

"Yes. Just because I don't have a man in my life doesn't mean I'm alone. They just can't seem to get a grasp on that. It's making me feel so…"

"Trapped."

This time, when she looked at him, it was with relief.

"Exactly! I want love and I want romance and I want to find someone who makes me feel all of that warm, gooey stuff they say that love is supposed to make you feel. It's all I've ever wanted, really. But…the fact that they're pushing so hard makes me feel so inadequate. So…so…"

He watched as she swallowed and offered a self-deprecating, awkward laugh. Idly, she tugged on her braid. "I'm talking too much, aren't I?"

"No. It's fine. Sounds like you don't often get to just talk like this. I know the feeling."

Thankfully, she didn't pry any deeper into that response. She only took another dainty sip of her wine and continued.

"Yeah, I really don't. I love my family, but I'm definitely the family therapist. Older child syndrome, am I right?"

"I wouldn't know. I was an only child." He shoved the peanut butter cup at the end of his tasting board into his mouth before he could elaborate on that any further. "So, what's all this about, then? What are you after? What do you want?"

"I want them to stop looking at me like I'm broken just because I don't have a boyfriend."

Cole's eyes narrowed, but in a good-natured way. "But something tells me you don't *want* a boyfriend?"

That was the contradiction he saw in her, anyway. Besides the fact that she'd already declared their current evening *not a date*, Annie Martin was the world's foremost bad matchmaker. Rose, who seemed like a pretty sensible woman, wouldn't have turned to her for dating help. Not real dating help, anyway.

"I want real, all-consuming, all-passionate love. Or I don't want anything at all. And because I haven't found the first…" She bit her lip. Cole leaned forward at the sight, telling himself it was more about the suspense of the moment than wanting to be closer to those lips. "I think I need to fake it. So, I had this plan. Well, half of a plan. Whoever Annie set me up with, I was going to offer him a kind of, you know…" She paused. "A fake relationship. He's in town shooting the movie, he plays nice for my family for a few weeks, we both get to protect our hearts and when he leaves town—"

"Your family gets off of your back about all of the love and romance stuff."

"Exactly. I've never really had a boyfriend here in town. If they see that I *can* have one…"

"Then they'll leave you alone. I get it."

What he *didn't* get was how this woman—pretty, agreeable, sharp-witted, intelligent—could be so accomplished and still worry her family so deeply over something as silly as her relationships.

"I also really, *really* need a date to my sister May's engagement party. When Harper, my other sister, got married, no one would shut up about the fact that I didn't have someone, and I'm not going through that again."

Their conversation lapsed into silence as they both sized one another up. Cole tried to understand the woman in front of him; she gazed right back at him with sharp, discerning eyes. Eventually, though, she returned to the task at hand.

"So, what about you? What's this research that you need help with?"

Moment of truth. He had only one second to answer the question, and his gut did the deciding for him. To trust her or not to trust her?

What choice did he have, really? Especially now, after she'd trusted him first? He swallowed, hard.

"Funny you should mention it. I actually—I'm keeping your secret here, so you have to swear you'll keep mine."

"Cross my heart."

Rose ran her fingers across the left side of her chest in a broad X. A gesture so cute, it almost set him off balance.

Cute? When did he ever think of things as *cute*?

"I'm having some trouble with my co-star. She's great," he lied, not wanting to drag a woman's name through the mud just because she was difficult to work with, "but we're not really landing in the chemistry department. Annie told me that you're something of a romance expert."

Rose barked a laugh, the sound sweet and warm to his ears. The second she stopped he wanted her to begin again. "Expert in romance novels and romantic movies, maybe, but I haven't really done the romance thing in real life. I think I just made that pretty clear."

"And there's something else, too."

"What's that?" she asked.

"You have to promise you won't tell Annie."

"I promise."

This wasn't something he'd told anyone. It was strange, trusting this information to a stranger, but if this was what he wanted, then he *had* to go after it. "You see, I am in love. Or, I was in love. I still love her, but she…I don't know. I guess she stopped loving me. And I thought maybe, you know, if I was seen around with someone, then maybe she'd realize what she missed out on."

"And maybe take you back?"

Cole nodded. "Exactly."

Was it the wine or something else that was currently making his head spin? Maybe the spark of light in her green eyes? The small lift at the right side of her smile?

"So, if you'd pretend to be my boyfriend…"

She trailed off, leaving him to think through the plan on his own. Yeah. This could work. A simple, businesslike trade. She'd get her family off of her back and get a date to her sister's engagement party; he'd get help with nailing his movie romance with Fiona.

And if the press—and Vivienne—just so happened to see him out and about in the cute small town, getting cozy with one of the locals, that wouldn't be so bad either. His heart beat a clip faster at the prospect of putting his recent breakup and the media fallout from it far behind him, of going full circle until he was back in Vivienne's arms.

The perfect crime. They'd both get what they wanted, and nobody would get hurt.

"Yeah. If you pretend to be my girlfriend. No emotions. No *real* romance. Just…you help me out with my movie stuff and with Vivienne, and I'll help your family believe that you're really falling in love."

For the first time in their little tête-à-tête, Rose Anderson seemed…uncertain. Nervous. Self-conscious, even. She twirled the stem of her wineglass, letting the dregs of her last sip spin in hypnotic circles at its base. Eventually, she braved a glance up at him from under her thick, light eyelashes.

"You think you're up to the challenge?" she asked.

"I don't think pretending to be in love with you will be any kind of great challenge."

He'd spoken before he'd really registered what he was saying. Still, he didn't regret it, especially when he caught her trying to stifle the first real smile he'd seen from her this entire evening. As he finished off his third tasting glass, Cole couldn't help but wonder how long it had been since someone had told her something like that. If he was in her life, he probably wouldn't have been able to *stop* saying things like that about the woman sitting across from him. But it seemed that no one else in her life had the same affliction.

He was surprised by how sad that revelation made him; the long drink of red wine didn't do much to help the situation.

When he looked up, Rose was staring disbelievingly down at the nearly empty glasses before her, drumming her nails on the table. Cole didn't blame her. They were perfect strangers entering into a strange and unusual arrangement with uniquely high stakes for both of them.

"I can't believe I'm doing this with Cole McKittrick."

"And I can't believe I'm actually buying into one of Annie's harebrained dating schemes."

"Oh, you don't even know the half of it. The last time she tried to set me up, she orchestrated an entire speed-dating night and tried to make it so that me and this guy would be the only ones who showed up."

"And what happened?" Cole asked.

"I figured she would do something like that, so I invited every single person I knew to come and join us for the night."

Someone who could outsmart Annie Martin? Cole couldn't deny that he was impressed. Not just by her story, but by the light in her eyes, the softness in her tone, the sweetness in her smile.

"Well, I think I just got myself a very clever partner in crime," he said, hoping she heard it for the compliment that it was. He lifted his final tasting glass to her in a toast. "To our fake romance."

Rose answered the gesture. "To our fake romance."

Their glasses clinked, and as Rose moved to return hers to her lips, their fingers brushed. Their skin only made the briefest of contact, but it electrified Cole as if he'd grabbed a lightning bolt by the tail.

Yeah, they'd come up with the perfect plan, he and Rose Anderson. All he had to do was keep up his end of the bargain and not fall in love with her.

He finished the last glass of wine in one gulp.

Chapter Five

Rose

There was a reason Rose didn't drink. She was the town's most notorious lightweight. Her most notorious dust-up saw her end up in a parking lot fist fight at the Bronze Boot and even now, years later, she still had to hear about it when she got in line at the grocery store checkout or was seen anywhere near alcohol.

So, when she woke up the morning after her date-not-date with Cole, her head pounded. Her entire body screamed for a good cup of coffee. She wanted nothing more than to throw her alarm clock straight into the nearest wall.

And that's when she remembered. Oh, right. In her slightly tipsy, slightly annoyed, slightly vulnerable, slightly erratic state last night, she'd agreed to fake date a world famous actor.

She couldn't even put the thought out of her mind because the second her sock-covered feet hit the hard wood of the landing, Harper, her younger sister, was upon her with a steaming cup of coffee and too loud, too enthusiastic conversation.

"So, how was your date last night?"

Great. So the entire house knew. That had been the point, obviously. Annie was incapable of keeping a secret but after the embarrassment that had been the almost-not-really date, Rose wished that her friend had suddenly learned to keep her lips sealed.

Or did she? After all, the whole point of her and Cole's arrangement was to make sure that her family got off of her back a little bit. Why *shouldn't* she revel a bit in stringing her sister along with that information?

"I thought this was a civilized house where we said things like 'Good morning' and 'Did you sleep well?'" Rose asked, her voice barely above a whisper despite the smirk that tugged at her lips. Loud noises rattled around in her empty brain, splashing around in all the excess wine up there.

"We usually are, but civility goes way out the window when Annie Martin knows my sister had a date before I do."

"Sh! Do you want Mom to find out too?"

Harper winced. Her voice immediately lowered as they made their way to the kitchen table. "Right. Sorry. But, Rose! How could you not tell me?"

Though Harper had gotten married and moved out of the house earlier this year she still managed the family's flower farm, which meant that these breakfast-and-chats were part of the morning routine, just as they had been for most of their lives. What Rose wasn't used to, however, was having the attention turned in her direction. She was the good one, the sister who never needed an early morning interrogation. That honor went to Harper and May, who'd gotten into their fair share of scrapes over the years.

But here she was, sitting across from wide-eyed Harper, who waited impatiently for her answer. The spotlight was on her now. No taking it off. She swallowed a big gulp of coffee and pressed her hands into the yellow-painted clay mug, hoping that the heat would steady her.

"It was a first date with some guy I didn't even know. After all of the false starts I've had, I didn't want to get everyone's hopes up."

That was close enough to the truth. Rose would leave the gossiping to Annie. She could hold the oh-so innocent high ground, while Annie did most of her dirty work for her.

Rose wasn't entirely comfortable with the idea of lying to her family. Liars were, in her opinion, the lowest form of people. But... if *Annie* did the romantic suggesting and all Rose did was hang out with Cole, then...that wasn't really lying, was it? That was just her family putting the pieces together on their own, wasn't it?

"Get our hopes up? Well, from the way Annie talked about it, my hopes ought to be sky-high. Come on. Tell me everything."

"There isn't anything to tell. It was a first date."

Again, half-true. A first date with *plenty* to tell. Just none of it that she could confess to Harper. Also, her hangover wasn't making her particularly talkative. But instead of shutting the conversation down these twin motivations actually stoked Harper's fire. She thought Rose was playing coy, something Rose had never done before in her life.

Never one to back down from an exciting story, Harper shook her head.

"There has to be *something* you can tell me. Did it go well? What was he like?"

"The date went about as well as an Annie Martin set-up could go."

"Oh, good Lord," Harper replied, her face drawing up in horror. "As bad as all that, huh?"

The thing about Annie Martin's matchmaking was that her enthusiasm didn't usually make up for her lack of talent in the field. She always selected wholly decent candidates, but ones who were also thoroughly incompatible with the person she was trying to set them up with.

The fact that Rose had felt anything for Cole McKittrick might well be the first big success in Annie's career thus far. Involuntarily, her hand clenched in her lap. She didn't want to think about how sparks had flown like rain when her and Cole's fingers had brushed last night.

She couldn't think about that. After all, he was in love with someone else, and even if he wasn't, Rose wasn't looking for love. At least, not from a strange, out-of-town actor who could turn his feelings off and on at will. Maybe she could trust him for the duration of their arrangement, sure, but she wasn't going to let herself go on feeling things for him.

"No, actually. Not bad. It was…He was a little standoffish at first, but he softened up after we got talking."

"Handsome?"

No sense in fibbing about this. Even if she did, eventually, Harper would discover the truth. "Heart fluttering. I've never seen a person that good looking in person. But you know I don't go for all of that hot guy stuff."

"Right. You're all about the heart. So, Shakespeare, what was he like on the inside?"

Interesting question. One Rose hadn't had much time to think on since getting home last night. As she took a long sip of her coffee, savoring the chicory notes on her tongue, she considered it. Cole McKittrick wasn't the kind of man she would have selected for herself out of a lineup, but there was something undeniable about him. Something that called to her, even when she didn't want to answer.

"He has lots of defense mechanisms. He's trying to keep people from seeing inside to who he really is, I think. But when he starts to let that guard down, he was funny. And kind. A good listener."

Better than a good listener. He'd been a saint to listen to all of her family drama. As far as Rose was concerned, that made him at least a decent person. Harper eyed her across the table.

"And what's his name?"

"Why, so you can stalk him on social media?"

A snort from her interrogator. "Yes, obviously."

Of all the information Annie had probably handed out like candy about this date, she'd left out the one piece of information Rose didn't want to approach. She fiddled with the teaspoon resting beside her coffee mug for a moment, buying her time as she tried to decide how best to make this confession. "Actually, I don't think you need to look him up."

Harper leaned forward. "Why? Do I know him?"

"Kind of."

"Spill, Rose. You're being weird."

"Err, well it's Cole McKittrick."

Harper blinked. The lines of her lips turned down, melting her beaming smile into a deep frown.

"Cole McKittrick? The man who *ruined* my favorite TV show?"

"He didn't ruin it," Rose scoffed, even as her stomach dropped to the floor. In her haze of thoughts connecting her new fake boyfriend with her sister's favorite show, she'd forgotten the hours upon hours of impassioned lectures she'd gotten when he'd left *Crime Spree: Beach City.*

Looked like she was in for another one. Harper's eyes widened in outrage.

"They *killed off* Blakely right after he'd been reunited with the love of his life and his illegitimate son, all because he wanted to quit the show! He ruined it. You know what? He's obviously a flake and a phony and he doesn't deserve you. I forbid you from seeing him again."

"Harper."

"Right. I'm sorry," she said, not sounding very sorry at all. Folding her arms across her chest, though, she tried to put on a brave, helpful face. "Are you…? Are you going to see the show-ruiner again?"

"I think so," Rose said, really leaning into the coy thing as she sipped her coffee.

But Harper didn't seem so conflicted. Instead, a broad, genuine smile took over her pretty face.

"Rose, I'm just…I know it's just a first date. Don't give me that look. But you seem kind of happy this morning. You've got a glow."

"I can't have a glow. I'm hungover."

Rose whispered that last word like she was confiding a great secret, but she was pretty sure anyone who saw her today would know right off that she'd had too much to drink last night. Harper winced.

"Broke your half-glass limit?"

"Afraid so."

Not to be deterred, Harper did something uncharacteristic of her. She tried to turn a negative into a positive.

"Well, maybe you were drunk on something else, too. Maybe you like this guy. Even if he is a horrible, TV-show-ruining hack who should never be allowed to make art ever again."

"You're really broken up about *Crime Spree*, aren't you?"

"Desperately."

They shared a laugh, and for a moment, it reminded Rose of the time Before. Before the Martins had come into town. Before all of her sisters and friends had fallen in love. When it was just them against the world. She'd never trade her sisters' happiness and romances for anything. But she *did* miss moments like these.

"Still," Harper continued, sounding suddenly more worldly-wise than any younger sister had the right to. "I'm excited for you. And *proud* of you. You haven't really put yourself out there these last few years. You've been so busy taking care of all of us that…I'm worried you haven't taken care of your own heart. I'm so happy that you finally are."

Suddenly, Rose's urge to throw up didn't have anything to do with her visit to the wine cave last night. Now it had everything to do with that sweet, wholesome look her sister shot at her across the table. The truth of the deal she'd made with Cole McKittrick now slapped her straight across the face. When she'd originally come up with her plan to get her family out of her romantic life, she'd thought about it in abstracts. As if her family were letters in a simple arithmetic equation. If she input a solution, into b family problem, then she would get c result. But now, as she stared back into her sister's warm, happy eyes, she knew it would be more complicated than that.

In her attempt to untangle her family from her love life, she would have to manipulate their emotions, making them believe in a romance that wasn't real.

"I didn't realize you were worried about me like that."

"How did you think I was worried about you?" Harper asked, narrowing her eyebrows slightly.

"I just thought you were just desperate for me to find a man so I wasn't alone."

"Well, I don't want you to be alone. But really, all I want is for you to be happy. That's all I've ever wanted. You're my sister, dummy. And if Cole McKittrick is going to make you happy, then maybe I can forgive him for ruining my favorite show."

"Thanks."

"But you should still tell him he's a monster for leaving *Crime Spree: Beach City*."

Rose rolled her eyes. "Yeah. I will."

Only…she wouldn't. Oh, she was going to talk to Cole McKittrick alright, but with every minute of her ride into town, she became more and more convinced that the topic of conversation wasn't going to be his long-running TV show.

Her idea had seemed so perfect last night, with a little bit of red wine in her belly and her shoulders bent under the weight of her family's expectations. But now, under the harsh light of the Californian sun, she realized that if they were going to do this, then they *both* would need some protecting. Some rules and guidelines to make sure that this thing didn't go south.

Instead of taking the family truck down to her flower shop in one of the quaint buildings on the town's main square, like she normally did at this time in the morning, Rose instead parked in front of The Hillsboro Grand Hotel. Just off of the main square, The Hillsboro Grand Hotel had been purpose-built a few years ago for all of the big-city tourists who'd started to come here to splash their cash around on the weekends, and according to the small card Cole had given her last night, this was where he was staying.

His instructions for getting in touch with him—visit or call the front desk of the hotel and ask for the name written on the card—weren't difficult, but the idea of going to the hotel clerk and asking to see "Superman," almost made her stomach turn.

Still, just a few moments after leaving her car parked on the front curb, she was in a golden elevator, being carried higher and higher until she reached the penthouse level. When the elevator slid open and she stepped out, there was one door in the small hallway.

Here goes nothing…

She knocked on the door. Waited. And when it finally slid open, her heart clenched. Her stomach dropped. And her lips parted.

Because there, framed by the doorway, stood Cole McKittrick. Dripping wet. And wearing nothing but a towel.

Chapter Six

Cole

He hadn't been thinking when he'd opened the door. But now, he couldn't *stop* thinking. Why was she here? Why had he answered the door with a towel around his waist? Why hadn't he just put some clothes on? Did she like what she saw? Why did it matter if she liked what she saw? Why was her jaw dropped like that? Why was she staring at the ceiling as if she couldn't bring herself to look at him? Why did he *want* her to look at him?

By the time the three seconds of stunned silence had passed between them, Cole had thought his way straight into a headache.

"You're naked," she choked.

"Only half naked," he protested.

"Right. Only half naked. And I'm going to assume you're wearing boxers under that, right? So it's basically like a swimming suit."

"It actually is a swimming suit. I just got back from the pool. It's not a big deal, really. We could just be on the beach somewhere."

"Well, not up here. It's too cold. You'd be wearing a wetsuit, but, yeah…"

"Yeah."

Oh, God. They were rambling. They were *both* rambling. Why was Cole's heart beating so fast? Why did he feel like he was going to throw up that heart if it didn't calm down?

He *never* rambled. Did the presence of beautiful women often make him nervous? Yes. Of course. His smooth on-screen persona was just that—a persona. Usually, he could turn it on in situations like this one, but today, he couldn't find the switch.

Especially not when Rose's eyes started to wander.

"You know what? I'm going to go into the other room and get changed."

Cole cleared his throat, then retreated from the open front door of his suite, trusting that Rose would follow behind him. He hoped that the sound of his hammering heart wasn't audible across the distance stretched between them.

"Yeah. Of course. Don't mind me. I'm just here to…Um…Wow, this is a really nice place."

It was. The Hillsboro Grand Hotel had given him the true star treatment, setting him up in the penthouse like this. His agent must have done a number on his contract to make sure he'd gotten the best room in the hotel instead of one of his co-stars. The suite contained three rooms and Rose followed Cole into a large living room area furnished with two plush couches and a wide dark wood coffee table. That connected to a small study that then connected to the bedroom and bathroom beyond. Cole made a beeline for that space, his head racing as he called to Rose behind him.

Clothes. He needed to get some clothes on. Then he could answer the other questions buzzing around in his brain. Questions like: what in the world is she doing here? Did she like the hotel room? Tossing on a pair of jeans and a loose sweater, he ran a hand through his hair to give it that rumpled, just out of bed look that his stylists thought fit his image.

"Help yourself to anything you'd like. Filming doesn't start for another two weeks and people keep sending me things so I'll visit their businesses. There's so much I can barely eat it all."

"And are you going to?"

"Eat it all? No, I usually donate stuff like that to a food bank—"

A soft chuckle from the other room told him that she'd at least partially forgiven him for the state of undress she'd found him in. "I mean are you going to go out to some local businesses?"

"Why? Do you have anywhere in mind? Could be a good way to spend one of our dates."

Dates. Such a strange word for what they were planning to do. Dating implied something romantic, something vulnerable, and both of them had agreed that they wouldn't indulge in anything of the kind.

Under other circumstances he might have been happy to date someone like Rose Anderson. But as it was, he wasn't here to find a new true love. He was here to win back an old one. Vivienne might have dumped him, but with this movie to relaunch his career, he was going to ensure that wasn't a permanent decision. He padded back into the living room, where Rose had made herself comfortable on the gold fabric couch.

Well, not exactly comfortable. She sat right at the edge of it, hands twisted in her lap and back ramrod-straight, as if she was preparing to bolt.

"Actually, that's what I came here to talk about. And I have to get away to my *own* struggling small business, so I should probably come out with it, shouldn't I?"

"Sure. What's up? You seem nervous."

Cole hadn't yet taken a seat nearby her, so she had to look up at him from under those long eyelashes of hers again.

"Well, you *were* naked," she reminded him.

The muscles in his lips twitched. "I thought we agreed I was half naked."

"Any amount of naked is enough to make a girl nervous."

"Your hands are naked. Should I be concerned you're going to seduce me?"

He sunk down to the chair beside her spot on the couch, the word *seduce* sticking in his throat. It had been a joke. If they were going to research together or whatever they were calling this, then they needed to be able to joke. They needed to be friends. Allies. But Rose seemed so tunnel visioned on whatever she'd come here to say that she didn't even laugh.

Probably better that she didn't. Cole didn't need any more incentive to think about Rose Anderson and seduction in the same sentence.

"I am *not* trying to seduce anyone. Especially after last night. I humiliated myself, talking like that to you."

"You didn't. But even if you did, I think we're even now. I saw you emotionally half naked; you saw me literally half naked."

Okay, he really needed to stop saying the word naked now. Even when paired with the word *half*, it made his mouth dry. And it wasn't helping this undeniable draw he was feeling toward Rose.

"I really think we need some rules."

"Rules?"

Rose pursed her lips, considering the room. Then, her eyes fell to the romance novels on a nearby table. "How many of those have you read so far?"

"One or two."

"Any fake relationship books yet?"

"Fake relationship?"

"It's a trope. Uh, in romance novels people have their favorite recurring story elements. Like a secret baby that brings the hero and heroine together, or a marriage of convenience that *starts* normal and professional, but eventually becomes anything but."

The way her voice lowered when she hit that last part made the lower part of his stomach tighten. She may have been teasing, but that didn't mean his body had to listen.

"Fake relationships are one of those tropes. And we're, kind of, you know, doing that right now. A fake relationship."

She stopped, but from the way she bit her lip, it seemed there was more she wanted to say.

"Okay…?"

"It's just that I wonder…you know, we're going to be in the middle of this thing, and we're going to be asking a lot of people to invest their emotions in us, and it just seems like we might want some rules."

Cole ran over her remarks a few times in his head before asking his follow-up question. The rules and logic of romance novels still didn't quite make sense to him.

"I'm not sure that I follow."

"Look, I know that we said last night that this was going to be a strict trade, but it just seems to me that in romances at least, when two people go into an arrangement like this that they…well…It's just that they—"

He didn't know much about romance novels, but he knew the look of a woman who didn't want to talk about her feelings.

"Fall in love for real?"

"Yes," Rose said, relief written across every inch of her face. "And if we can't make sure that our feelings are protected, then I don't think I can go down this road with you. I mean, you're an actor. You *know* how to make people believe things that aren't there and—"

She stopped herself. He waited for her to continue.

In her eyes, he could see that she was having the same internal battle now that he'd had last night. *Is this person worthy of my trust?* Eventually, when she'd made her decision, she squared her shoulders and looked him in the eye, steadfastly holding his gaze.

"A long time ago, I was lied to by someone I thought I loved very, very much. The details don't really matter, but it broke my heart. I'm just worried that if I go down this road with you—"

Light bulb. That explained everything. "Then maybe you'd get hurt again."

"Yeah."

Cole bit down hard on his bottom lip. He needed Rose's help with his research; he needed Rose's help to convince the tabloids he was totally over Vivienne Matilde. But he wasn't a monster.

"If you don't want to continue, then I understand. But I can *also* understand wanting all of that stuff you said you wanted last night. To be free of your family's expectations. To get a date to your sister's party."

"And I do want it. Really, I do. I just—"

He searched his mind for some kind of compromise, some way to make them both comfortable and their consciences clear. Because in that moment, the thought of her walking out of his hotel room door never to return?

That sent his thoughts scrambling, grasping for straws that might keep her there.

He didn't know why. They'd had one meeting and she'd spent the first half of it not liking him very much. But there was something there. A spark. A tension. Maybe the beginnings of a friendship. He didn't want to lose that.

Believe it or not, he didn't have many friends to spare right about now.

"Okay. I'm in. Rules. What would you like the first rule to be?"

Rose considered him for a moment, and then: "Number one. No lying. We'll be together. We'll go out in public. But we won't tell people we're dating. We'll simply let people draw their own conclusions."

She'd unclenched her fists in her lap and relaxed slightly back into the couch where she sat. That seemed like a good sign. Reaching to the small table beside his chair, he grabbed the hotel stationery and pen so he could jot this down. He wanted this to work, and despite the fact that he'd only known her for a few hours, he wanted this to work with Rose. After all, who else in town would be willing to agree to a no-strings-attached fake dating scheme?

"Okay. That seems fair. Any others?"

"No kissing. And no dancing. No more half-naked meet-and-greets at the door. Physical stuff like that is *always* how these romance novel things start."

His tongue itched to point out that if that was the case, then they were probably well on their way to falling in love, considering she'd already seen him without his shirt on, but now didn't seem the time for joking.

"Oh!" she interjected, her face very grave, very serious. "No skinny-dipping."

Cole's pen hesitated above the sheet of hotel letterhead. Skinny-dipping? Those two words coming from her pretty, pink lips did things to him he didn't want to admit. He swallowed hard.

"Do you think it's necessary to write that down?"

"The Miller's Pond is a popular date spot in town, and it's known for skinny-dipping. I think adding it to the list is prudent. Just in case."

"Okay." He dragged his pen across the paper, adding the new rule to their list. "No…skinny…dipping. What else?"

For a moment, they both considered their next step in silence. Cole tried to keep his attention on the paper in his hands instead of on the woman across from him, who somehow made knit eyebrows and intense concentration extremely alluring. By the time she spoke again, he realized he'd been thinking more about her than about the task at hand here.

"No family dinners," she said, with a little nod that sent locks of red hair tumbling over her shoulders and her electric blue glasses slipping slightly down the bridge of her nose.

"You have family dinners?"

"Every Sunday night. If you go, it'll be too many questions that we don't have the answers to. Should the occasion arise, you've got to have an excuse ready."

"I think I can handle that."

He added it to the list, writing slightly slower than he had been before to buy himself some time. Family dinner. She actually had dinner with her family every week? A pang of jealousy plucked at his heartstrings. His own family wouldn't go see his movies, much less bother to see him in person.

The rule made perfect sense. He wouldn't break it if it meant that they could keep up their charade. But now that he knew about the existence of these family dinners, he couldn't help but want to go to one, to see what it was like to have a big, warm family to share meals with.

Cole cleared his throat. No use thinking about it. "Anything else you want to add?"

"No real feelings," she said, pushing her glasses back up the brim of her nose. "Nothing too heavy. I don't want a repeat of last night's sob-story performance, okay?"

"Now wait a minute. I'm supposed to be learning how to fall in love with someone. That's the whole point. If I don't learn anything about you, how am I supposed to—"

A secret, teasing smile pulled at her lips. She raised one eyebrow in his direction, the universal sign for *I'm about to burn you with my words.* "It's called acting. Maybe you should try it sometime."

Her sentiment was perfectly reasonable. If this was supposed to be nothing more than an exchange of services—his boyfriend-ing for her help in his romantic research—then keeping their relationship strictly professional would ensure that their business didn't hit any unwanted snags.

But still...when he thought about last night, sitting across from her at the wine bar as they traded quick conversation, and of her here today, having come to visit him just so she could try to protect her family's feelings, a picture of who she was began to form in his mind. Incomplete, sure, but a beautiful picture all the same. The thought of his relationship with her being romantic was impossible. But the thought of not even being her friend didn't sit well with him.

"What about *no falling in love* instead? No real feelings seems like a bit of a stretch. Besides, what if we become lifelong friends after this?"

She rewarded him with a laugh, but the edges of the sound rattled with bitterness. "Yeah, I can see it now. Rose Anderson, the lonely spinster and Cole McKittrick, the high-flying international superstar. Still friends at fifty."

"Who says you'll be a spinster? And who says I'll still be a star? I saw a run-down goat farm for sale a few miles out of town. Maybe I'll buy that and give up on the whole acting thing."

He offered her a laugh of his own, but when he looked up to meet her gaze, her smile was brittle. Skeptical. For reasons he couldn't even begin to fathom, he suddenly wished he could take back the joke.

"One more rule," she said.

"Yeah?"

"Let's be completely honest with each other. No false hope, okay?"

Cole's smile slipped. *No false hope.* It stung. But he couldn't disagree with that one. Onto the list it went.

"Yeah," he agreed. "Deal."

Chapter Seven

Rose

Once Rose reminded him that she needed to get to work, Cole offered to walk her there, saying that perhaps she could even give him his first romantic hero lesson on the way. Before they'd left, though, he'd grabbed a bag of lemon cookies that Rose had been eyeing, tossed them to her, and winked like they were sharing some intimate secret.

Okay. So Cole McKittrick wasn't that bad. Maybe, he was even a little bit good. Not that she was interested in him or anything, not beyond their business arrangement anyway. But it was more than the handsome smiles and the cookies. Rose had known plenty of men who wouldn't have heard her out, who wouldn't have talked through her concerns with this plan and offered compassionate solutions.

Cole had. And that won him a heap of points in his favor.

It didn't hurt that his body made her mind wander into distinctly romance-novel territory.

No, Rose, she reminded herself as they stepped into the tight, antique elevator outside of his penthouse, *focus on the task at hand, not the man at hand.* It was easier said than done though when he stood so close to her, smelling of firewood and salty sea air—she'd have to ask him about his cologne; his scent was completely bewitching. She couldn't even imagine creating something so complex in her own perfumes—but still, she made a valiant effort, doing what she usually did when she was nervous.

Rambling.

"So, you said you have two weeks before you start filming? Well, I really don't think that's going to be a problem at all. Two weeks is plenty of time to fall in love with someone. Or pretend to, at least. Or, understand what it feels like to fall in love with someone. Come to think of it, why don't you just rent a few Nora Ephron movies and just copy whatever Tom Hanks does? I mean, no one could ever *really* emulate Tom Hanks, given that Tom Hanks is a once-in-a-generation human being, but—"

In the confined space of the elevator, she couldn't ignore the way his carved, larger-than-life body turned toward her, effectively pinning her up against the left-hand wall.

"Rose…" he asked, narrowing his eyes slightly in amusement, "are you nervous?"

"What gave it away? Am I sweating?" She stiffened. "Oh, no. It's worse than that. I'm oversharing."

Really, Rose? You asked him if you were sweating? No wonder she hadn't been able to find true love yet if that's how she talked to men she had even the slightest interest in. Cole, to her surprise, didn't press the next elevator button and make a break for it, leaving her behind. Instead, he chuckled.

The sound warmed her from the inside out.

"Just a little bit. But don't worry. It's strangely endearing."

"So, what do you think?" Rose prompted, not wanting to dwell on the endearing comment. "About my Nora Ephron idea? You wouldn't even need me at all. Just rewatch a few of those and—"

"I've never seen a Nora Ephron movie once, so rewatching it will be a pretty big challenge."

The elevator *dinged* their arrival into the lobby. Good thing, too, because if they'd still been traveling, Rose might have pulled the emergency stop and made the man watch the digital copy of *You've Got Mail* she kept on her phone.

"Never seen a…" She shook her head to clear it. Insulting someone for never having seen her favorite movies wasn't an especially kind thing to do. Besides, what wouldn't *she* give to go back and see her favorites for the first time? What a treat he had ahead of him, seeing Tom Hanks and Meg Ryan fall in love. Striding confidently out of the elevator and into the hotel lobby, the beginnings of a plan formulating in her mind. "Alright. Well, I know our first date, then. We're renting some romantic comedies and we're having a movie night."

"Are there any romantic comedies with explosions in them?" he asked, sidling up beside her as they took to the sidewalk outside of the hotel.

"Men. You're all so obvious, aren't you?" She rolled her eyes, though she couldn't deny the allure of adding some car chases to *Kate & Leopold* or *His Girl Friday*. "Tell you what. I'll throw you a bone and we'll watch *The Mask of Zorro* and *True Lies*, too."

For a few paces down the sidewalks of Hillsboro, they walked in silence. Rose took the opportunity to drink in the sights and the sounds of her hometown, her favorite place in the world. Tight-knit and passionate, the community had poured everything into Hillsboro, filling the storefronts with well-loved shops and high-quality goods. But it was the people that made the town what it was, and on a day like today, when folks waved at her from across the street and smiled when she passed, she knew this was her home. The place where she belonged.

Annie had told her hundreds of times that she wasn't going to find love in a small town like this. That the dating pool was simply too shallow, that by the time a woman was Rose's age, her chances were all gone. But if the choice was between a fairy-tale romance and her home, the choice was easy. Hillsboro was part of her. No man was worth ripping out a piece of her very heart.

Eventually, the silence lapsed. From the corner of her eye, she watched as Cole's smile turned into a triumphant smirk, as if her silence proved something.

"You still haven't answered the question."

"What question?"

"Are you nervous?"

Oh. Right. That question. Well, no point in lying about it. She'd already overshared about her personal life and her sweating. Might as well completely ruin all respect he had left for her.

"Yeah. I told you. I haven't done this dating thing in a long time and—"

"Speaking of. Do you want to elaborate on that? Don't you think I should know about whatever terrible heartbreak destroyed Rose Anderson's romantic prospects forever?"

Her back straightened, like it always did when she thought of the past. "I'd tell you, but the story would probably bore you to death. It's a tale as old as time."

At that moment, they arrived at the northern stretch of Hillsboro's Main Square, where the Anderson family's flower shop sat. It was a humble storefront set into a street of historic buildings. The sight of the white-painted façade and the gold and black letters painted onto the front window loosened the knot tightening the space between Rose's shoulder blades. This was home. Her turf. And while Cole might have been able to throw her off of her game back in his hotel suite, he wasn't going to be able to do the same here.

Rose had been only nineteen when she'd taken over the tourist-facing branch of her family's flower farm, selling carefully curated bouquets and wholesale bushels to anyone who walked through her front door. Despite her young age, she'd discovered she had a knack for composing poetry with peonies and poinsettias, for writing sonnets with sweet peas and snapdragons. Here, in the quiet of her shop, with its towers of flower display buckets and her chalkboard walls with the special sales of the week, she felt she could truly be herself.

It's why she didn't say anything more about her romantic past. This was the place she went to get away from all of that. Her romantic past wasn't quite as tormented as some, but the brush with heartbreak in her college days had been enough to spook her off of unnecessary entanglements almost entirely.

Cole was the first second date she'd had since then.

"I see." He smiled, knowingly. "You want to keep your secrets. I get that. Now, what are we doing here? Is this the part where I learn the language of flowers and meet some hard-nosed shopkeeper who reluctantly grows to appreciate me and my fun-loving ways?"

"I thought you said you didn't watch romantic comedies?"

"I get the formula."

Withdrawing the key to the shop from a ring in her purse, Rose officially opened up the shop for the day. The moment the door swung open, the scent of fresh-cut flowers and thick twine barraged her senses, washing away the dust of the day. Here, everything was fresh. Every flower was a new opportunity, a new chance to create something beautiful and bring a little bit more happiness to the world.

Leaving Cole almost as an afterthought in this world of hers, her body went into autopilot, running through her usual list of pre-opening chores. Lights on. Computers on. Check the flowers. Inspect the orders list for the day.

But one of those chores, she decided, was a perfect place for Mr. Cole McKittrick to start his romantic hero training. Plucking the broom from where it lived behind her counter, she tossed it over to him. He caught it with the ease of someone with a personal trainer on speed dial.

"Well, no. You're not here for a life lesson. You're here to sweep."

"…What?"

"First lesson of falling in love? Sometimes, it's hard work."

Cole's jaw dropped. Rose's heart stuttered. Had she offended him? But then, his face transformed into an appreciative smile, and he offered her a little bow, like an equal acknowledging an equal.

"You totally conned me," he gasped.

"You're the one who wanted to keep up this charade. If you want the real girlfriend experience, sometimes you've just got to do back-breaking manual labor."

Tucking herself safely behind the counter, she went through her to-do list for the day. Not many pick-ups were scheduled for this afternoon, but with plenty of fall events coming up, she'd need to start planning her bouquets now. Did she have time to sweep the floors herself? Absolutely. But would it give her great pleasure to make herself a cup of coffee, sit behind the counter, and make a celebrity do it for her?

Also, yes.

"Is this because I answered the door half naked earlier?" he asked.

Rose fought back a blush, and offered back a teasing volley of her own. "No, it's so the customers on the street can see you in the window and be drawn in to buy some flowers. You're a one-man curb appeal."

Under his breath, he muttered something that sounded suspiciously like "I bet Tom Hanks never had to do this," but she could tell he was still in good humor. Playing along.

The muscles in her stomach danced at the thought. Maybe this arrangement of theirs wouldn't be so bad. Maybe he was right. Maybe they would be friends at the end of this.

She tried not to dwell on how warm that thought made her.

Unfortunately, Cole turned out to be less than handy with the sweeping. She hadn't noticed before, but he'd apparently slipped one of the romance paperbacks into his jeans before they'd left the hotel, and every so often, in between the chores she assigned him, he'd take a "break," leaning against the wall or lounging on a crate so he could get in a few more pages.

At one point, he practically threw the book on her counter in frustration, clearly annoyed by something he found there.

"Okay, so here's what I don't get."

"Shoot," Rose said, unable to keep the smile out of her voice.

"Why don't any of these people just talk to each other? It seems to me that if they all just sat down and said their feelings, that things would turn out alright."

Ah. So he was one of those people. Rose didn't even have to consider her rebuttal. She'd thought over this particular point countless times.

"Why doesn't the villain in a James Bond movie just kill him instead of going on and on about his plan? Because it's a story, and we'd rather it be interesting than logical."

"It doesn't bother you?"

No, it really didn't. Maybe it had once upon a time, when she'd first started reading romance novels, but now…she was a grown woman with her own fears and wants and secrets. She knew that not everything could be solved with an easy conversation. Sometimes, protecting your heart was worth it.

Besides. He didn't exactly have any room to talk.

"Cole, with all due respect…You're doing all of this to try and make a woman jealous, so she takes you back again. Why don't *you* just go and talk to her, hm? Every woman wants to be wooed with words."

Cole's expression faltered. As if he was surprised by what she'd just said. As if he was surprised by his own reaction to it.

"She's…Well, Vivienne isn't…She's just…It's more complicated than that."

"Care to elaborate?"

Before he could, a familiar, high-pitched voice shrieked as the bell over the front shop door rang out her entrance.

Annie Martin was here.

"Rose Anderson! Cole McKittrick!" she squealed, practically sprinting into the shop. "I can see that your first date went pretty well, didn't it? What did I say? Didn't I tell you that this was going to be simply fabulous for the two of you?"

"Mm-hm," Cole grumbled, flashing a conspiratorial look in Rose's direction.

Annie slipped her sunglasses away from her eyes and waggled her eyebrows suggestively as she made her way to the counter. "How's the *research* going?"

"Great, actually. Rose is teaching me about the love language of flowers right now," Cole snarked.

Usually, Rose knew how to handle Annie. She was an aggressive creature, but not a particularly complicated one. All you had to do was speak slowly, speak calmly, and not make any sudden movements in the direction of romance and, eventually, she would back away.

But there was something about Annie's approach today. Something about the stare she fixed squarely on Rose. Something about Cole's proximity and the fact that he looked at her as if they were really in this together.

"And we're going out on another date tonight," Rose blurted.

Cole blinked up at her over Annie's shoulders. He didn't even have to say what he was thinking for Rose to figure it out. *I thought the first rule of this arrangement was that we weren't going to lie.* But still, when Annie spun to face him, he shrugged nonchalantly, playing along coolly so as not to rile Annie any further.

"Yeah. Movie date. Romcoms. You know."

If Annie noticed anything was amiss in this picture, she didn't let it show. Instead, she clapped her hands together and gave a little spin of excitement. "Ah! I love it when a matchmaking scheme comes together. Hey, tonight is game night for George and I with Harper and Luke. They're all coming over to my place. Why don't you go to Luke's and have a movie night? He's got the big outdoor projector."

Rose paused. There were three things wrong with that. One, since when were the couples having date nights without inviting Rose? Two, Rose didn't want to imagine sharing a romantic night with Cole under the stars. And three, Annie didn't live with Luke anymore. It wasn't exactly her house to offer.

"Are you volunteering your brother's house for him? Like, without his permission?"

"He won't miss it. Besides, I'm the one who found and rented us that house all those years ago. Without me, none of this would have happened, so he owes me."

Rose knew better than to argue with the pint-sized planner, so she just slapped on a smile and made a mental note to call and clear things with Luke and Harper before she drove over there.

"Sure, Annie. That sounds great."

"Perfect! I'll leave you two lovebirds to get better acquainted then and text you the details later!"

With the clicking of her heels and the *ding* of the door's bell, Annie was gone, leaving Rose dizzy in her wake. While she tried to get her bearings once again, Cole strode over and leaned against the counter, looking more like a romance cover than any real-life man had the right to. Once again, she caught a whiff of that scent of his, which wrapped around her and begged her to move closer to those flexing muscles of his.

"So…" He drew the letter out and raised one eyebrow. "You're pretty good at this fake dating stuff, huh? That was a pretty slick plan you came up with."

Rose shrugged and tried to hide her blush.

"Listen, you keep reading those romance novels, and one day, *maybe*, you'll be as good at fake dating as me."

And while part of her hoped he would, another part of her hoped he'd never even get close to her level of expertise. After all, she was already swooning and blushing *now*. She wasn't sure her heart could take it if he got any better at this.

Chapter Eight

Cole

They'd set their movie night for seven thirty, and Rose had promised to bring the popcorn. After a day of sweeping up small scraps of leaf from her shop floor and plowing through the stack of romance novels he'd bought from the bookshop in the corner of the square, he realized that the excessive workouts the studio had put him through to make him look TV-ready hadn't prepared him for small-town life…or sweeping. He hadn't minded the work. It was different than what he'd been used to, but there was a certain charm in having helped Rose with her shop. And getting to sit behind the counter on a high stool to read his books all afternoon had given him the chance to watch her without her being completely aware of it. The quiet page turns of his Regency—a word he'd just learned today—romance novel eventually faded into part of the shop's background noise, until it seemed she'd completely forgotten about his existence.

Cole was fine with that. It had given him more of an opportunity to watch Rose in her natural environment. What he saw didn't exactly surprise him, but still, it stuck with him even now, hours after they'd parted. She was soft-spoken and easy-going. Kind to even the rudest customer, patient with the ones who had no idea what they wanted. Every time a child walked in, Rose greeted them with a small daisy, free of charge, as a souvenir of their visit. When customers were sparse, she turned to the brown butchers paper on the counter, where he watched as she sketched out arrangements and design ideas, blossoming full bouquets in nothing but permanent marker doodles.

And when she was thinking very, very hard, she bit down on her bottom lip in such a way that Cole suddenly lost all control over his breathing patterns.

Not that it mattered, of course. No, these were all just observations. Nothing that would affect him personally. It was nice to have a partner in crime, but she couldn't distract him from his goal. From winning back Vivienne.

Hours later, in the car, as he drove towards his appointment with Rose, Cole couldn't remember the last time he'd been on a real date. Vivienne hadn't really been into "date nights," at least when she didn't think there would be a camera around. And he found he couldn't remember the last time the thought of a date had made him *nervous*. He was an international star, a celebrity who faced down cameras and paparazzi almost every single day of his life. The thought of spending a few hours with Rose Anderson and her mane of red hair shouldn't have been enough to cause a lightning storm in the pit of his stomach. Yet, as he drove up to the address he'd been sent for tonight in the car the production team had rented him for the duration of the shoot, he couldn't help tapping his hands against the steering wheel anxiously.

"What are you doing? What is that noise?"

The thoughts of his date had *also* distracted him from the hands-free phone call with his manager he'd gotten roped into. In most other circumstances, Cole didn't mind chatting with Blake, his agent, but today, for the first time in a long time, when Cole had seen the caller I.D. pop up, he'd been tempted not to answer it.

"Erm…Nothing. Just tapping on the steering wheel. I'll stop. So, what's on your mind?"

After all, Blake never called just to chat. There was always an angle or an agenda.

"Do you get the tabloids up there? Any internet connection? Can you see the tweets?"

"Yes, Blake. I can see *the tweets* up here," Cole said, trying to keep the sardonic notes out of his tone and failing miserably.

"Well, I think you and I need to get on some damage control about this whole *you know who* thing."

Vivienne Matilde. They still weren't saying her name. A few days ago, he'd been grateful for that particular quirk that his entire team—from stylists to press agents to his manager—had adopted, but now, it irritated him like a fresh poison ivy rash. But while he could believe that his manager still wasn't saying his ex-girlfriend's name, he *couldn't* believe the other stuff coming across the crackling phone connection.

"Oh, *now* you want to do damage control? What happened to 'all press is good press?'"

"That was then. This is now. Besides, you're the one who didn't want to tell the truth, though God only knows why."

God probably did know why, but he wasn't the *only* one. Cole *also* knew exactly why he was doing this. For one thing, he wanted

Vivienne back, and he wasn't going to achieve that by dragging her name through the mud and telling the truth about what had happened between them. And for another, the truth didn't exactly make him look very good, either.

"Well, I'll have you know that I'm way ahead of you on that front."

"Yeah, you got this movie," Blake said, apparently not picking up on the subtext Cole was laying down. "And I'm glad we landed you that. It's good, but we can't wait for the movie to come out to generate good press and goodwill. I think we need to start developing alternative ways for you to make headlines *now*—"

"Blake, I told you. I'm *way* ahead of you."

Cole wasn't exactly proud of the way he'd gotten ahead, and the plan hadn't actually been his. More of an accident of fate. But still, for once, he was taking an active role in his own life and career. After years of having everyone else call the shots, he was finally figuring stuff out on his own.

He wanted at least a little credit for that.

Credit, though, wasn't in his future. Not from Blake, anyway, who started chuckling on the other end of the line.

"Pray tell, then. What's your big plan out there in the sticks? Don't tell me. You're going to curry goodwill with the movie-going public by dating some provincial out there. You're going to sweep her off of her feet like some kind of Small-Town Cinderella—"

Small-Town Cinderella. Those three words conjured up images of Rose in a ball gown, her hair swept away from her lovely face and her body wrapped in fabric that clung in all the right ways, but the disparaging tone shoved shards of invisible glass down his throat. This wasn't a conversation he was interested in having anymore.

"Oof, Blake. I'm sorry," Cole said, raising his voice and doing his thinnest impression of someone struggling through rotten cell quality. "I can't hear you. Getting up into the mountains here. Bad reception."

Blake didn't buy it. "Don't you hang up on me—"

"I think I'm going to have to call you back. Later. Sorry, bye!"

The protest from the other end of the phone line continued, but Cole ended the call before the expletives could begin.

Ten minutes later, he arrived at the Martin house. He should have guessed that Annie Martin, certified social media influencer, and her tech mogul brother, would have lived in the nicest house in town, but *nice* didn't quite cover it. Palatial mansion would have been a more accurate descriptor than "house," but really, the domicile wasn't even the piece of the landscape that held his attention.

The house rested at the top of a sweeping hill, which usually must have been covered in greens but was now filled with a tapestry of changing fall colors. Even in the glow of the moon and the illuminated house, the hill looked like it had been painted over by a great impressionist doing a color study. It was more artwork than reality, but artwork that he could reach out and touch if he rolled down his window and stretched just beyond his car. He didn't really think of himself as the romantic type to get all moony-eyed over landscape, but it seemed that Hillsboro—or a certain flower expert, who'd encouraged all kinds of fanciful, romantic thoughts in him—had already gotten under his skin.

There was still one thing about this countryside Cole couldn't get over, and that was the stars. Out here in the country, where the light pollution was basically non-existent, one glance heavenward rewarded him with the most beautiful tapestry of light and space. After spending so many years in Los Angeles, he'd almost forgotten that stars also existed outside of the realm of science fiction and the sight of so many entranced him.

When he was done gawking, Cole parked at the top of the hill and strode up to the house, where the illuminated porch called to him.

"Rose? Rose, are you around?"

But by the time he'd called her name, he'd found her, sitting on a porch swing, completely surrounded on all sides by low-laying tables and wine crates, each of which were covered in candles and a truly astounding display of food and wine. The glow of the candles danced across Rose's face, which deadpanned at the sight of him. That meant there could be only one explanation for this over-the-top date night extravaganza. Cole winced.

"Annie?"

"Yep," Rose confirmed, setting aside a television remote she'd had in her hands and putting all of the focus on the tables surrounding her. "All Annie. Well, actually, I think my sister had something to do with it, too. She bought my favorite kind of pie."

Against his better judgment, Cole's eyes darted excitedly around, searching for the item in question. He was aware that his excitement probably made him look ridiculous, but he didn't care. He wanted a slice of that sweet, sweet good stuff.

"There's pie?"

Rose quirked a surprised eyebrow. "Is that exciting to you?"

"When I used to film *Crime Spree*, I'd spend ten months out of the year eating nothing but protein shakes, chicken breasts, and leafy greens," he said, picking through the tables so he could sit beside her on the porch swing. "For a month before heading out here to film this movie, I spent every night before bed researching all of the places I would go and eat once I got here. Hillsboro is quite the culinary hotspot, you know."

"Well, you're in for a treat, because Millie's Pie Joint makes the best pie in the world. Fact. If you're going to break your diet, this is the pie to do it with."

Almost as soon as Cole had taken the seat beside her, he regretted it. The porch swing had looked *way* roomier from across the porch. Now, he couldn't escape her proximity or the heady floral scent of her. In the chilly fall night, her warmth made him want to draw even closer than they already were. She quickly cut them both slices of a gooey peanut butter and chocolate coconut pie, and they settled back in for their first bites.

The flavors hit Cole's tongue like the first drip of water to a dying man. He audibly moaned, unable to help himself. Rose giggled beside him, the free sound echoing down the hill beyond the porch.

"It's good, right?" she asked.

"Good? There isn't a word to describe this pie. Good is an *insult* to this pie."

"Millie's Pie Joint is iconic in Hillsboro," Rose said, through a mouthful of coconut whipped cream. "We'll have to go there ourselves. Very good date spot."

The moment the words hit the air between them, Cole knew that they had been accidental, so casual that she'd forgotten what was really going on between them for a moment. But then, she swallowed, her face went pale, and she turned to explain herself.

"I mean, a *not*-date date spot—"

"Don't worry. I know what you mean." Cole started to explain to her that he didn't mind using "date" as a shorthand, but a small, stray swipe of sweet cream on her left cheek distracted him. "Hey… you've got a little something—"

Before he realized what he was doing, he'd retired his slice of pie to a nearby table. With a gentle, slightly shaking hand, he reached up with his thumb and brushed away the mark. His breath quickened. Their eyes met. He didn't want to move, didn't want to break this contact.

"Oh, thanks," Rose said.

Their eye contact held for a few seconds too long. Cole cleared his throat and pulled away, happily going back to his pie and trying not to think about how close his thumb had been to her lips or how soft her skin had felt beneath his touch.

"So, what's on the movie lineup for tonight?"

Rose seemed as eager for the distraction as he was. Scrambling to put her own pie aside, she once again grabbed the remote she'd been fiddling with upon his arrival. A few button presses later, the awning of the porch before them began to lower, revealing a viewing screen, and a panel in the wall behind them opened to reveal a flickering electronic projector. Fake rocks hidden nearby played a sweeping jazz score as the menu screen of the film in question flickered to life.

"I thought we would start with the 1934 Academy Award Winner, *It Happened One Night*. Clark Gable. Claudette Colbert. The fabled walls of Jericho."

He didn't know what any of that meant, but she seemed excited about it, so he wasn't going to burst her bubble.

"It's in black and white," he countered, gently.

He hadn't been joking when he'd told Annie that the only black-and-white movie he'd watched was *The Wizard of Oz*.

"It's a classic. And believe me, aside from the parts where it doesn't hold up, this movie *really* holds up. Besides, black-and-white movies look really spectacular under the stars."

Cole's voice faltered for a breath. He didn't know about the movie, but he knew that Rose certainly looked spectacular under the stars. "Well, with a recommendation like that, how can I refuse?"

A brisk hour and twenty-seven minutes later, Cole's sides hurt from laughing. Truth be told, he'd never really been into movies. He'd mostly been picked for his role in *Crime Spree* because a casting director thought he was charming and looked good with his shirt off. Black-and-white movies and art-house films had never exactly been his style, but there was something charming about a head-strong woman and a rogue having to fight for their own love story.

There was also plenty charming about the way his movie partner gasped and laughed and whispered fun facts to him throughout the whole thing.

But that's what got him, really. Now that he'd seen her movie and read more of the books she liked, something nettled him. It didn't make sense. As they picked at the remains of their picnic, he couldn't keep it inside any longer. If they were going to be friends and get through this charade together, then they were going to have to talk about it.

He needed to understand her.

"Can I ask you something, Rose?"

"About the movie? I think I've given you all of my fun facts already."

"No, actually. About you."

All around them, the crickets hummed their evening serenade and the stars twinkled, watching and waiting for her reply just as he did. Eventually, she shrugged.

"I guess that would be alright."

"Why movies? Why books? You clearly love this romance stuff. Why not go out and find your own story like this?"

Maybe he was overstepping his boundaries here. And he knew the night before that she'd given him plenty of reasons why she hadn't done it. But still, he could feel that there was something else, something she was hiding or fighting.

"It's the same old story, I guess."

"And what is that?"

She smiled, a slow and secretive one that made him feel like she was teasing him. Like, *well, if only you'd read more romance novels, then you would be able to guess.* Instead of responding, though, she asked a question of her own.

"What about you, hm? You could have anyone in the world. Why do you want to get this one woman back?"

Cole opened his mouth, confident that an answer would come to him easily. But the longer he thought, the fewer things he had to say.

"You know, we were both on the ascendant. Together for a few years, lived together, did the whole thing. She was building her career as a model; I was working on *Crime Spree.* We did everything together. Parties, engagements, fundraisers, photo shoots. All that stuff. She had big plans for our future at the time. She and I made sense," he finally said, settling.

Rose's eyes immediately darkened. Her smile vanished.

"Oh."

"What's that supposed to mean?"

"Nothing. It's just…that's not the same thing as love."

Chapter Nine

Rose

Rose thought about Cole that entire night. She couldn't get those thoughts out of her head. *She and I make sense.* In all of the romance novels *she'd* ever read, the man who wanted to win back the heart of the woman he loved could—and often *would*—go on for pages and pages and pages about the woman he loved. But Cole had just said *we make sense.*

That wasn't the same thing as love. That wasn't even the same thing as affection. That was just…sad.

Rose promised herself that she was going to get to the bottom of it, to understand him better. There was something going on with Cole and this woman, and she wanted to know what it was.

When she went down for her usual breakfast and coffee the next morning, she wasn't greeted by Harper's exuberant peppering of questions. Instead, she was met with nothing but the sound of a stirring spoon clinking against the smooth sides of a mug…and her sister's familiar sighs. She paused at the top of the stairs, and the hesitation was enough to finally earn her a call.

"Rose? Is that you?" Harper's voice traveled up the staircase, a summons she couldn't ignore.

"Yeah, I'm coming."

A moment later, Rose was in her usual spot at the table. A cup of coffee in her hand and a stack of printed web articles strewn across the table. For a long moment, neither Rose nor Harper spoke as Rose's eyes wandered over the various pictures. Some were grainier than others. Some appeared way more scandalous than Rose remembered being last night. But they all ran under similar headlines. *IS COLE MCKITTRICK FINALLY OVER EX VIVIENNE MATILDE?*

Heat burrowed beneath Rose's skin. By now she had to be pink as a camellia in spring. The date—not a date, a *research trip*—last night had been almost perfect. They'd stayed up later than she'd anticipated, talking and laughing and debating the finer points of how the famous screwball comedy they'd just watched could apply to his own movie-making career. This time, she'd mercifully stayed away from the wine, so she knew that everything passing between them had been real. It had been a wonderful night. Which, by the laws of the universe, meant that it was only natural for all of it to get ruined so quickly after.

Well, ruined was probably a strong word. After all, she and Cole *had* wanted this to happen. They'd wanted to make Vivienne jealous. But there was only one person in the world she could think capable of something like this. Only one person in the world who would even *think* to do something this brazen and outlandish, and it was the *who* of the betrayal and not the *how* that burrowed under Rose's skin and stayed there.

"So, do you think—"

Harper didn't even need to finish that question. Yes. Yes, Rose did think.

"Annie set us up. She had to. I know she did."

Her stomach revolted at the thought. Hot bile rose up in her throat. But it only made sense. Annie knew all about the power of the press—hell, she was dating an investigative journalist—and she'd been the one to make the "magical" night happen for them. All of this had been her idea. The pieces fell easily into place. All the pieces except for one. Annie was supposed to be her friend. A real friend wouldn't have done this to her.

Annie had done a *lot* to meddle in her life, but this was something entirely different.

From her place across the table, Harper narrowed her eyebrows and leaned forward, rustling some of the newspapers as she did.

"…And you're mad at her about that?"

"It was my private date. She sent cameras to my own personal evening with someone, and now—"

"Now people are going to know that Rose Anderson might actually be feeling something for someone?"

Rose tried to understand what was happening here, but so much was being thrown at her all at once she could barely manage it. Her best friend had ratted her out to tabloids—tabloids that Annie was supposed to hate!—and now her own sister was trying to convince her that it wasn't such a bad thing? Rose could hardly get her words of shock out past her gritting teeth. A hot anger flashed through her.

"You're on *her side*?" she stammered.

Harper paused, apparently trying to figure out how to best approach her argument. Her eyes fell back down to the papers before them.

"It's a few pictures in the paper. If you'll remember, that's part of how Luke and I fell in love."

"Yeah, but we're not in love. We've been on *one date*—the one in these pictures—and now the entire world is going to know about it."

"So?"

So, my friend shouldn't have wanted to meddle in my love life! She should have trusted me to handle things on my own.

But, of course, Rose couldn't say any of that out loud. Just like she couldn't say the *other* worry she had out loud. *Because now, I'll never be able to forget Cole McKittrick.* Originally, Rose had been planning to live out this Cole chapter of her life, and then turn the page as soon as he left, forgetting him and the bargain they'd struck as quickly as possible. That was best, she thought, for her heart. But now, she would always have to think of him; she'd always have evidence of the night she spent laughing and talking on the porch swing as Claudette Colbert and Clark Gable fell in love. That night she spent wondering if he and Vivienne Matilde were really as right for each other as he seemed to think they were.

"You're impossible," Rose muttered. She had to be running a fever by now; her blood was almost certainly boiling beneath her skin. "I can't believe you're taking Annie's side in this."

"I can't believe you're overreacting like this. Where's the calm, reasonable Rose we all know and love?"

In a split second, with that one question, something inside Rose snapped. Up until now, she'd loved being the calm, level-headed sister. The smooth rocks against which everyone else's chaotic sea crashed.

But now, she felt years of pent-up emotion bubbling to the surface. Years of shoving aside her own feelings and desires to make room for everyone else's. Before she could stop herself, those feelings poured out of her.

Cole had liked her passion. Her stories. Her variable nature. Why couldn't everyone else who was supposed to love her?

"Have you ever considered that the reason I have to be so calm and reasonable is that you and May and Annie are so reckless? If I joined the chaos brigade, the world would probably implode."

Harper paled. An apology was written all over her face, but Rose wasn't in the mood to hear it.

"Rose—"

"I'm going to talk to Annie. If you see them, tell Mom and Dad I won't be home for dinner."

Half an hour later, after a stop to get an iced coffee in the hopes that it would settle her nerves and cool her anger (it hadn't), Rose found herself at the door of Annie's small townhouse in the center of Hillsboro. Unlike the mansion she used to share with her brother, the one where she'd sent Rose and Cole last night, this wasn't a beautiful abode. It was *cute*.

And right now, that cuteness, with its multi-colored façade and slightly crooked mailbox, only served to stoke Rose's fury. Annie made her living on cute. Her entire personality hinged, at times, on her cuteness. But that cuteness could sometimes be a mask, a mask she used to conceal her slightly *less* lovely qualities. Like her tendency to meddle in other people's lives.

Without pausing to consider or to take a few deep breaths and control her emotions, Rose rang the doorbell. Inside, she heard the whistle of the teakettle and the barking of Annie's dog, Monster. The normal sounds of the house. Rose wasn't sure what she'd been expecting. Annie surreptitiously ending a call with some shady paparazzi folks? Hushed conversations about how to expose their next date?

"Rose!" Annie said, when she eventually threw open the front door. As usual, she looked perfectly put together, magazine cover ready. Her usual uniform of pressed silks and bright florals still held up this morning, despite the fact that Rose had snuck up on her here. And her smile was so broad and bright that, for a moment, Rose almost forgot that it was fake. A distraction. "How lovely to see you. Though I am surprised that you don't have your new beau on your arm—"

"Come on, Annie," Rose said, her voice low and shaking. "You know I'm not here for a social call."

"Whatever do you mean?"

As Annie turned to let Rose into her house, she asked that particular question with a shaking voice that mirrored Rose's. Only, her shaking voice sounded like it was coming from uncertainty rather than anger. Following her friend inside, Rose kept her eyes down. Not because she didn't want to take in all of the sweet accents Annie had used to give the old place a bit of a modern flair, but because she couldn't stand to see all of the framed pictures Annie had used for decorations around the house. Pictures that chronicled their friendship. Everything from their first sleepover (back before Harper and Luke were even friends, much less a married couple) to their time together as bridesmaids in Harper and Luke's wedding were represented, and everything beyond and in between.

"You sent the reporters to Luke's house, didn't you? You offered us your brother's place so we'd be in a controlled environment, so you'd know where to send them."

Annie's jaw hung open. Her hand froze around the pitcher of lemonade she'd just picked up. Even as Monster nipped around at her heels, tail wagging, she didn't take her wide eyes off of Rose's face.

"…I can tell by your expression that you aren't here to thank me."

"Why would I thank you? You invaded our privacy."

"For the greater good!" Annie said, her voice rising defensively. "Come on, Rose. I know you. I know you're just trying to get a date for your sister's engagement party, but you *deserve* someone who is going to stick around! You know that you aren't really one to hold out with any relationships. You get set up, you go on a date, and then you retreat back to your quiet, small world. After you told me you wanted to try again, I didn't want you to spook. I thought that maybe you and Cole just needed a little push to stick together for a while, to see if it could work in the longer-term. If you were all over the press, I thought you might not be able to hide from your feelings. From each other. That's all."

The heat beneath her skin hadn't been helped by the iced coffee; she was burning now, all hot with righteous anger.

"You are *such* a meddler."

For the first time in their friendship, Rose didn't mean it as a teasing compliment. She meant it as an insult. Probably because, up until now, Annie's meddling had been harmless. Overbearing, but harmless. Now, the stakes were astronomically high.

Then it hit her. Cole. Oh, God, in all of the mess of the morning, she hadn't even thought to call him. She'd been in such a rush to chew Annie out for what she'd done that she hadn't even stopped to worry about him. They'd done what they set out to do—get some press that could make Vivienne Matilde, star model and international glamour girl, jealous. But was that *really* the best thing for them? And what if Cole didn't want to see her anymore now that they'd gotten what they were after?

The color drained from Rose's cheeks. Her entire body went ice cold now. Her condition didn't improve when Annie flashed her a timid smile and nudged her like the old friend that she was.

"I just want you to be happy, Rose. I may not always go about it the right way, but there's never a moment where I'm not just trying to help you be as happy as you deserve."

Rose's tone remained bitter. "There's a lot of that going around these days. Did it ever occur to you all that I know what I'm doing? That maybe I know how to make myself happy more than you all do?"

Once the emotions came pouring out of her, Rose found them nearly impossible to stop. She loved her sisters. She loved Annie. She loved the bonds that they'd grown into over the years and how much they all cared about each other and fought for each other. But she resented the fact that they didn't trust her. Not even with something as basic as her own happiness.

In that moment, the steel around her heart hardened.

Slowly, Annie sunk to one of the high, re-upholstered bar stools lining her kitchen counter. She dropped the lemonade pitcher perhaps a little too harshly along the fake marble surface.

"So…" she said, dragging the vowel out as she avoided Rose's gaze. "I guess I shouldn't tell the press about your next date?"

"You won't get the chance. Because I'm not going to tell you about our next date."

Not until she'd talked to Cole first, anyway. He should have been her first stop today, *would* have been her first stop, if only she hadn't let her emotions get the better of her.

Annie, never one to have a normal reaction to anything, actually brightened at this dismissal. She was incapable of looking at anything but the sunny side of bad news.

"But you *are* going to see him again?" she asked, a little bit too excited.

"If he still wants to go out with me after this. Yes."

Annie's smile only grew. Her confidence came flooding back. "Oh, don't worry. He will. He'll definitely still want to date you."

As usual, Rose didn't need to ask about Annie's blistering confidence. That was just her friend's way. Annie was confident in everything, especially the things she wasn't certain of. But Rose did wonder if her friend had inside information in this particular case.

For the rest of the afternoon Rose counted down the minutes until she saw Cole again—not that she was looking forward to seeing him again she told herself. No, she just…eagerly awaited getting on the same page with him about their future. That was all. She turned Annie's words over and over again in her mind: *He'll definitely still want to date you.* But how could Annie be so sure? And what business did she have being so confident?

It was Rose's life. She was so tired of everyone having it figured out when she didn't even have the first clue.

Chapter Ten

Cole

Good work, kid. The press is having a field day over these pictures! I'd like to see Vivienne get this much good press!

All morning long, since those pictures had surfaced on the internet, Cole's phone had been vibrating with messages just like that one. Congratulating him for something he hadn't even done.

When he'd woken up this morning and seen the papers he'd been confronted by a sea of mixed emotions. First, as usual when he heard there was a headline about him lately, dread. For as long as he could he tried to avoid the newspapers in front of his hotel room door and he kept his phone and laptop safely stored away. But there were only so many cups of coffee he could drink and only so many times he could reread the same scenes from his script before he *had* to brave a look.

What he saw caught him completely by surprise. Surprise that the paparazzi had found them, surprise that he'd been so wrapped up in Rose and the movie that he hadn't noticed their presence out in the darkness beyond the screen. Surprise that, for the first time in a long time, the press about him was leaning towards the positive.

There was triumph, too. The photos were just the kind of thing that might make someone jealous—all cozy, romantic and lovely. Even the fact that they were clearly grainy and taken through a long-range telescopic lens didn't erase that effect. In fact, it only heightened it. Now, it looked like he and Rose were in some kind of secret, forbidden romance, one that they were trying to hide from the public that might corrupt their love.

Vivienne was going to have a field day when she saw this.

Sunday afternoons meant that Rose's shop would be closed, and last night they'd decided to meet at the farm for their next "date," which she'd promised would come with a full curriculum for their upcoming meetings. When he hadn't heard from her all morning despite sending a handful of texts, he could only hope she still wanted to see him.

Had she run for the hills when she saw the paparazzi headlines? Would she still want to keep up this charade after experiencing the limelight firsthand? He didn't know, but he *did* know that he didn't like the thought of not seeing her again.

She was fascinating. A contradiction. He wanted to unravel her, to get to know her better. The thought of leaving the mystery of Rose Anderson unsolved was impossible.

The Anderson Flower Farm couldn't have been any more different than the Martin home where he and Rose had spent last evening. Where that place had been high-tech and modern, fitted out with every luxury money could buy, this was a working farm and rustic in every sense of the word. The house at the top of their hill was nestled into the center of yawning fields of growing flowers, each stretching out towards the sun as they tried to gulp up the last of the warmth before winter set in and crept into their petals. A rusted-out barn and slightly broken fences completed the picture, but as slightly worn around the edges as the place was, Cole got the sense that it was well loved and well looked after.

It looked like a home. In his last years of chic rented houses in the Hollywood Hills and hotel rooms, he couldn't remember the last time he'd been in one of those. His chest tightened as he fought off thoughts of his *own* family and his own home.

He didn't think about the truth of his past very often. He avoided the subject when he could help it. His official biography told everyone who would listen that he was a home-schooled nobody from some nondescript part of Los Angeles. The truth was a lot more complicated, and his home was as far from the glittering, bright lights of L.A. as it was possible to be.

It was also, apparently, pretty far from the Andersons' house. This place looked like it was built on love. And while he'd once thought about his home that way, too, now he knew better.

As always, it proved better to pretend. Pretend he had some nice family waiting for him. Pretend he had everything Rose had. Pretend he wasn't pretending.

Pulling up to the house, he counted three cars in the driveway—all beat-up, secondhand trucks. Strange. Rose had told him they would be the only ones out here today. Cole parked and pulled himself out of his rental car, scanning the homestead for any signs of his date for the afternoon.

He didn't find her. He didn't have the chance. Because almost as soon as he slammed the car door behind him, a giant, white, fluffy monster barreled across the wide field in his direction, all hideous, growling barks and bared teeth.

Cole froze, his fight-or-flight instincts not quite making their decision yet.

Thankfully, just when it seemed that the dog was close enough to pounce, a short, squat, perfectly lovely woman with a short-cut brown hairstyle intercepted, snatching the dog by the collar and leading it away so she could tuck it inside the nearby barn.

"Stella! Stella, no ma'am! Stop it! Oh, I am just so sorry about her, she's usually better around…" The barn door slammed. Cole's shoulders slackened. The woman rose to her full height and met his eyes with a curious, delighted expression. "Strangers. But you're not a stranger, are you, Mr. Cole McKittrick?"

"I'm sorry to barge in like this, ma'am. Rose and I were—"

From her age and the slightly reverent way with which she spoke to him, he could only assume that this was Rose's famous mother, the one who wouldn't stop pushing her towards romance.

"I know all about you and Rose. Not from my daughter, of course, she likes to play things very close to the chest, but I *do* read the papers and let me just say, sir, that we are so happy to have you here filming a movie in our little town. And we are so happy that you decided to spend some of your time with our Rose. How are you finding it?"

Cole blinked. That was a lot of information to take in in such a short amount of time. "Hillsboro is great. A wonderful…" he searched for a word that he thought might please the woman currently staring at him with wide, excitable eyes, "…very, you know, American town—"

The truth of the matter was that it was only just starting to grow on him. It was quaint and cute, but everyone who'd warned him about spending too much time in a small town had been right. He *did* miss the creature comforts of Hollywood.

Not that it mattered. Mrs. Anderson waved her hand dismissively in his direction.

"Now, how are you finding Rose? Is she behaving herself? We would just love for you to come to dinner tonight, meet the family. I'm cooking—"

Once again, Cole found himself saved by a member of the Anderson family. This time, by a curvy woman with a braid and an exasperated look on her face who appeared from within the barn where the dog had just been banished. For some reason though, Cole got the distinct impression she wasn't upset at the barking animal, but at her own mother.

As much as Cole had wanted to see Rose just a few minutes ago, now, he was *desperate* to see her.

"Mom, what are you doing?"

Mrs. Anderson held out her hands in a defensive posture, her gaze flickering between the woman who'd just arrived and him, as if waiting for him to defend her. "I'm just talking to Mr. McKittrick here, Harper."

Harper. Yes, that was one of Rose's sisters. He remembered hearing about her now. The middle sister who was married to Annie's older brother. She adopted a sarcastic smile, which she focused squarely on her mother.

"I think Mr. McKittrick is here to see Rose. Not you."

"You see how my daughters treat me?" Mrs. Anderson joked, laying it on thick as she gave Cole her full attention now. "No respect at all around this place. I can't believe I raised children like this. Honestly. Anyway, it was so nice to meet you finally—"

"Mom!" Harper urged.

"I'm going. I'm going. No need to be rude in front of our guest."

As the fall wind whipped around them, the slightly terrifying Mrs. Anderson took her slow, lumbering leave. As if guessing at the older woman's game, Harper waited until she was out of earshot to cast him an apologetic glance and offer her gloved hand for a shake. Cole took it, gratefully. Mrs. Anderson clearly meant well, but being in her presence felt a bit like being stuck inside a maraca during a rowdy mariachi number.

"Hi. I'm Harper. Rose's younger sister."

"Nice to meet you, Harper. I've heard a lot of great things about you. I'm really sorry about barging in like this. I didn't know anyone was going to be here—"

"Oh," Harper said, raising an eyebrow and starting off, forcing Cole to follow behind her. "So you thought you and my sister were going to have some kind of secret tryst?"

"I promise you, that's not what I—"

"Look. She really seems to like you."

Cole didn't like the way his chest tightened at that particular revelation. "She does?"

"Yes. And Rose doesn't let herself like a lot of people. She's the kind of person who's always friend*ly*, but never a friend, if you catch my drift."

He wasn't entirely sure he *did* catch her drift, actually. Rose hadn't been friendly when they'd first met—she'd been snarky and annoyed and as scared of him as he was of her—but now it felt to him like they were becoming fast friends.

Was he misreading the signs? Was she just being polite to him while he was over here, stupidly thinking she was his friend? He didn't like the way those questions made him feel, like he was desperate for her approval. He should have been ready to keep his eye on the prize—on Vivienne. He shouldn't have cared how his partner in this arrangement really felt about him. But he did, all the same.

As they came around the back of the homestead, they reached a small exterior building, one of the six that made up the complex—a home, a barn, a storage space of some kind, an office, and this. Harper stopped and leveled a threatening, deadpan look right at him.

"So, basically what I'm saying is that if you hurt Rose, I *do* have access to an incredibly sharp, three-ton threshing machine."

Cole blinked. "Did you just threaten me?"

"Let's just say that you ruined my favorite TV show. If you break my big sister's heart, I can't be held responsible for what happens. And if a jury of my peers is stocked with fans of the show in question, there isn't a court in the world that would convict me."

"This got very intense very quickly," Cole muttered.

"Rose is my best friend. And *Crime Spree: Beach City* really was my favorite show."

There were tinges of humor dancing in Harper's tone that kept him from thinking she'd go completely slasher film on him, but the set of her jaw and the tightness in her shoulders told him she wasn't fully joking, either. Not that it mattered. He had no intention of breaking Rose's heart, nor she of letting him. That was part of the reason they'd come up with their rules. So neither of them would end up hurt by the end of this little charade of theirs.

"I promise I won't hurt her. And who knows? Maybe one day we'll do a reunion special or something for *Crime Spree*."

"The only thing I hate more than someone who hurts my sister is someone who gets my hopes up with no intentions of following through."

Wow. She *really* didn't like the fact that he'd left the show.

"Right. Well, it has been quite an auspicious meeting, Harper Anderson. I'm glad to have met you. And I'm really sorry about the show, but—"

His attempts to extricate himself from this conversation were interrupted by the swinging of the door in front of them and a familiar voice.

Finally. Rose. He'd found her. Standing in the doorway, hair down, face flushed, and eyes bright, she looked more than beautiful in the afternoon sunlight. She was striking.

"Harper, what are you doing out there—?" That's when she noticed him. Her frown lifted up into a smile. "Oh, hey, Cole."

"That's my cue to leave," Harper muttered, turning on her heel. "You two enjoy the Smell Shack, you lovebirds."

The Anderson family was an interesting bunch, that much Cole now knew. With a mother as sharp-elbowed as Mrs. Anderson and a sister as protective as Harper, it was a wonder that Rose turned out halfway normal. Still, he could feel in their interactions how much they all loved and cared for one another, which was more than he could say for most of the people he knew.

Once Harper was gone, he raised an eyebrow, confused by a certain turn of phrase that had been carelessly tossed out into their conversation.

"The Smell Shack?"

Rose waved at the small structure, inviting him inside. From the exterior, it looked like one of those tiny homes or a "she shed," that he'd seen in commercials sometimes, but once inside, he felt as if he'd stepped through the wardrobe or the looking glass and into a more magical world. Part laboratory, part potions chamber, the golden light peeking in through the homemade curtains gave the entire set up an otherworldly quality. There were cozy chairs and low tables tucked into one of the corners. Fancy glass bottles and boxes of handwritten labels. A standing chalkboard at the far end of the room.

"I crush the raw ingredients for perfume and do all of the chemistry back here. That's why she calls it that. Sorry in advance if you get a headache. And I am just…" She flushed pink, as she waved out to where her sister had just been standing. "I hope Harper wasn't giving you a hard time out there. She really loved *Crime Spree*, you know?"

"No, it's fine. Man, perfume, huh? That's a pretty neat hobby. Do you sell this stuff anywhere?"

She shifted uncomfortably beneath his gaze.

"Sometimes in my shop, or in May's old store. But it's just a hobby. A thing I like to do on the side."

Something in her expression told him that wasn't the whole story, but he didn't want to push it.

"I, uh, thought that your family wasn't going to be here today? Isn't that why we agreed to meet up here?"

"Yeah. That's what I thought, too. But after the papers and everything, Mom wasn't about to leave me alone and Harper decided to come in and get some work done in the barn. Or so I've been told."

Cole helped himself to one of the chairs as Rose busied herself, cleaning off the countertops in her witchy laboratory. The assault on Cole's senses—everything from vanilla to lavender to brown sugar to ambergris—didn't distract him from the bitter note in her tone or the way her eyes narrowed slightly when she said her sister's name.

"You don't seem happy about the familial closeness."

"You don't want to hear about my family drama."

"Rose, we're friends. You can tell me what's happening in your life. That's what friends do."

For a moment, only the clinking of perfume bottles answered him. He held his breath. This was a moment of truth, a moment to see if Harper had been right when she'd said Rose liked him.

"Shouldn't we be talking about our sudden international notoriety?" she eventually asked.

"I don't have anywhere to be if you don't. We could talk about both."

"I love my family."

"No one could ever doubt that."

In fact, he was jealous of how deeply her family cared about her. How much she cared about them, in turn.

She focused intently on her tidying, scrubbing at surfaces that already shone and fiddling with already perfectly straight jars.

He recognized that look. Not from their previous encounters, but from one of the romance novels he'd read. It was the look of someone who didn't often get the chance to be honest with someone else. The look of someone on whom everyone else depended, but who rarely got to depend on anyone else. When she spoke again, she confirmed that his romance reading had paid off. He was right.

"But I've spent my entire life taking a back seat to them. To all of them. And for a long time, I was totally content with that. I liked being in the back seat, never having to think about where the road of life or whatever was taking me. I was just…along for the ride, I guess."

"But…?"

"But now, I realize that giving them the keys for so long has made them believe I don't even know how to drive. That I don't even know where I want my life to be heading. They're trying to set me on this one, singular path and I want to go a different way, but they just don't understand it. They want me to fall in love, and of course I want to fall in love, but I want to do it my way. And *not* because someone thinks the only way I'll be happy is with some guy. Does that make sense?"

The sunlight from a nearby window painted itself across her smooth skin, shimmering as dust motes danced like magic through the breeze. Now, it wasn't just her shack that had an otherworldly glow; she had it, too. But that glow didn't only come from the outside, it came from within her. Her face settled into a determined kind of expression that could only come from someone trying to wrestle their own destiny from someone else's hands.

His admiration for her grew exponentially. This wasn't just about her trying to get her family off of her back in regards to finding a boyfriend. This was about her feeling like she wasn't a marionette on the end of someone else's strings.

"You want some control over your own life again."

"Oh, it's so embarrassing," Rose said, a self-deprecating smile cutting into her words. "I just turned twenty-eight and I don't even know how to steer my own existence."

"It's not embarrassing. It's always going to be a push and pull between you and the people who love you. I think that's only natural."

"You're speaking from experience?"

A challenge. A dare. One he didn't know if he knew how to answer. His mind flashed to thoughts of Vivienne, then to thoughts of his own family. He brushed both of them aside.

"I think we were busy talking about you."

"What happened to friends listening to each other?"

He considered that for a moment. True, it wasn't fair for him to ask her for her secrets if he wasn't willing to share his own. "Let's just say that you aren't the only one trying to finally get some control over their own narrative. Speaking of which: what about the stories in the paper? Are you okay?"

At long last, Rose turned away from her counter, leaning on it and giving him a full view of her. He was grateful for her honest face; she couldn't keep anything a secret, not even if she wanted to.

"It's what we wanted, isn't it? I guess I was just surprised it happened so quickly. And that Annie was involved."

That was what got him about this whole thing. Annie *never* liked the press. The fact that she was currently dating a journalist shocked him enough, but to actually give them a tip? To encourage their blood-hounding ways? It seemed too much, even for her.

"She doesn't meddle just to meddle or because she likes control or anything like that. She wants us to be happy. She's delusional, of course, but she thinks you and I could be a *real love story*."

A fresh stab of feeling entered Cole's heart. Annie wanted what was best for both of them; she was a good friend in that way. But she believed that Cole's best course forward was to forget about Vivienne completely, to move on and find new love. He disagreed. He knew he'd only be happy if he got her back, if he proved his love to her and if she finally confessed her love right back.

From the corner of his eye, Cole caught a glimpse of someone moving out in the brush beyond the window. A short, stout, now familiar figure. He needed to act fast. They had a spy in their midst. Reaching up, he gently brushed away an imaginary lock of hair from Rose's cheek. Only when Mrs. Anderson turned to leave did he remove his hand.

"What was that for?" Rose asked.

"Your mother was lurking by the window. I didn't want her to get suspicious."

"Oh. Right. Of course. Thank you."

"My pleasure."

And it was. It had been his pleasure. She was so soft, so sweet, so tough and so touchable all at once. She awakened feelings in him that he hadn't imagined ever feeling for someone else. Not after Vivienne.

Rose cleared her throat, ducking away from him and heading straight to the blackboard at the back of the shack.

"So. A curriculum. I promised you a curriculum, didn't I?"

"I think there was some discussion of planning out our lessons, yes."

"Well, that box over there is where you start." She pointed to a crate on the floor, which practically overflowed with paperbacks. "I saw what you were reading yesterday, and they're all great, but these should supplement your learning. Besides the books, we're going to focus on four areas of romantic chemistry."

With a flick of her wrist, she sent the blackboard spinning, until it landed on its other side and revealed a thorough lesson plan written out in precise, white-chalked handwriting. *ROMANTIC CHEMISTRY 101* read the heading. Cole let out a long, low whistle. Impressive.

"You really have put a lot of thought into this, haven't you?"

"Well, I had a lot of time when I was trying to distract myself from the avalanche of text messages asking me if I'm really dating Cole McKittrick."

He couldn't quite tell if she was bitter or pleased about having to reply to those rumors. He also couldn't understand why he felt so twisted-up about the idea of her being bitter about it. Instead of offering any kind of clarification, she turned towards the blackboard and began talking him through the bare bones of the plan.

"So, the four areas. Shared experience. Shared story. Shared interest. And..." She cleared her throat, cheeks turning pink as she glanced down at the floor beneath her. "Shared physicality."

Cole's jaw hung open. He blinked. His mouth was suddenly dry as a desert. Words escaped him. Shared physicality. The words struck through him, hot and devastating as a lightning bolt through a tree.

"And I know one of our rules was to avoid this, so I completely understand if we want to strike, you know, uh, hands-on learning from that portion of the curriculum. But in a visual medium like film, if you're not able to muster physical chemistry, then no one is going to believe you, so we could, um, watch, uh, more films, basically. Study the way that the pros do it on screen and—"

"Hey," he said, noticing she was doing the nervous rambling thing again. His question was out before he could stop himself and hold it back. "Do you think I wouldn't want to kiss you?"

"Cole, I think we made the rules so I wouldn't have to ask myself questions like that."

The air between them tensed. Cole did the only thing he knew how to do in a situation like this: he pretended it hadn't happened and moved on as fast as he possibly could with a smile.

"Fair enough. So, where do we start?"

Chapter Eleven

Rose

It took practically an Act of Congress to successfully rescue Cole from the clutches of her mother that night. Sundays were for family dinners, yes, but as far as Mrs. Anderson was concerned, "family" also included potential candidates for future sons-in-law that she wanted to interview. Eventually, though, Rose claimed a stomach ache and begged off of dinner entirely, meaning that Cole could escape her mother's attentions—which he, strangely, didn't seem to mind—and Rose could avoid having to face Annie and Harper.

She knew seeing them both again was inevitable. They were her best friends. Nothing would ever change that. Still, she needed time to lick her wounds and grow out her backbone a little bit.

Thankfully, the night gave her plenty of time to think and plan. During their time at the farm, she and Cole had talked about the upcoming film production and the potential problems he saw with it. Well, Cole talked about it while Rose asked the occasional prodding question and mostly tried not to think about how hard she must have blushed when she mentioned *physicality* in his presence.

Truth be told, the idea of kissing him didn't *not* appeal to her. He was handsome and kind and funny and it seemed like he genuinely liked spending time with her. That was more than she could say for most of the guys who'd come around her in the last few years.

But she knew that even if she was in an emotional place to start a relationship—which she wasn't, especially considering her belief that love would find her, not the other way around—a relationship with Cole McKittrick was impossible. Sure, he was a decent enough human being to be nice to her and to help her out in this bind she was in with her family. But that didn't mean he was going to fall madly in love with her and sweep her off her feet and spend the rest of his life with her, whispering sweet nothings in her ear and giving her goosebumps the way he had when he took her face in his hands.

He was famous. They were from two different worlds. He was in love with someone else. And more than all of that, he played pretend for a living. Rose had been burned by liars before; she didn't need to put her feelings right in the hands of another one.

No, she and Cole were going to be friends and that was that. Nothing else to it.

She was just packing up for the night to go out and see her new friend when the bell jingled over the door, announcing the sudden appearance of Marshall Barnett, the older, blind gentleman who ran the town's best grocery store, Barnett's. At the sight of him, Rose instantly dropped her bag and her jacket and set to work getting the man's usual—a bouquet of sunflowers.

"Hiya, Rosie!" Mr. Barnett practically crowed as he made his way across the tiled floor towards her counter. "Hope you aren't closing up yet!"

"Nope, just about to, but I think I can squeeze you in. Getting your usual, I assume?"

Monday evenings, Mr. Barnett always came to the shop on his way home from work to collect the flowers for "his best girl," who also happened to be a one-year-old black cat he'd rescued from a garbage can outside of his store. Rose always counted it as one of her favorite customer interactions of the week.

"Gotta keep my girl happy, you know. Say, word around town is that you're dating some kind of...uh...person?"

"Cole McKittrick's in town. We're just..." Rose paused as she wrapped butchers paper around the bottom of the arrangement, letting the crinkle of the paper buy her some time to think of an appropriate explanation, "...we're just hanging out."

"Ah, hanging out." Mr. Barnett chuckled and handed over the usual cash for this exchange. "I remember when I used to be young enough to hang out."

"Is there anything else I can get you, Mr. Barnett?" Rose asked, not unkindly. She would have been lying to say she didn't suddenly want this interaction to come to a quick end. Mr. Barnett was one of the town's most notorious ears to the ground; he was also one of Hillsboro's best people. The last thing she needed was his involvement in this scheme of theirs.

"No, ma'am. But I think there's something I can do for you."

"And what is that?"

Rose steeled herself for another batch of homespun, cutesy advice. As if she didn't get enough of that at home. Sure enough, she got what she expected in abundance.

"Give you a little piece of wisdom, one I've learned from my many, many years of life. When life offers you an opportunity, you should take it."

"Did Annie put you up to this? I know you two are like peas in a pod now that she's dating George."

George, Annie's boyfriend, was the son Mr. Barnett never had. It would have made sense for Annie to try and weasel her way back into Rose's life via her favorite Monday appointment.

Mr. Barnett held up his hands—cane in one, flowers in the other—as a way of announcing his surrender. "No one had to put me up to it. I hear a lot of rumors in my line of work, young lady, and I barely ever hear them about you. I'm no good at math, really, but even I can put two and two together there. Rumors indicate risk. And it doesn't seem like you've been taking a whole lot of risks in your time."

"Thank you for the advice, sir. I'll take it under consideration," Rose said, glad that he couldn't see how fake her smile was.

Who did he think he was, anyway? What, now strangers thought that they had the right to come in here and give her advice on how to live her life? Didn't anyone in this town know that *risk* meant just that? Risking her heart, risking her safe, even-keeled existence? Besides, she *couldn't* take a risk on Cole McKittrick because there was no risk to take.

They were in this together, but they weren't together and they weren't going to be. There was a kind of safety in that, in experiencing the trappings of romance, but never being threatened by it. He was trying to win back the woman he loved. She was trying to stay away from love until she knew it was real. End of story.

A small, traitorous voice in the back of her head whispered, *that's not true, is it?* Her stomach sank as the memory of their time in her workshop came flooding back to her. When he'd looked at her, eyes full of honesty and surprise, and asked, *do you think I wouldn't want to kiss you?*

He seemed so sincere in that moment. But he was an actor. And Rose didn't trust herself to know when someone was telling her the truth. Not when it came to romance. Not anymore.

"And Rose?" Mr. Barnett asked, breaking through her reverie.

"Yes, sir?"

"You really should give Annie a chance to apologize. She told me she feels awful about what she did with you and the paparazzi folks she called."

Ah, yes. She should have known this was about more than Cole McKittrick. Annie Martin always had a way of sneaking back into her life. Well, this time, she wasn't going to let that happen.

"I'll take that under consideration, too."

Once Mr. Barnett left and Rose collected her things, she followed her extensive close-up procedures, flipped the *Open* sign that her sister, May, had carved for her years ago, and stepped out onto Hillsboro's Main Square. If her store brought her comfort in times when everything felt like one giant mess, the square at night was almost as good a balm to her chaotic heart. She loved the lazy dancing of the wind, the sound of quiet conversation from couples sharing ice cream or slices of pie by the fountain in the center of the square, the clinking of glasses and laughter from the restaurants down the street. Now, with fall creeping up steadily on them, she loved the sensation of sinking into her sweater and being cozy there.

Tonight when she stepped out she realized that, for the first time in a long time, she wasn't alone out here on the sidewalk. Usually, this side of the square only saw customers at the far corner, where Millie's Pie Joint sat and slung slices to hungry mouths well into the evening, but this evening, a tall, handsome someone stood there, waiting for her with a warm, flustering smile.

"Nice evening, isn't it?" Cole asked.

"What are you doing here?"

"Don't we have a date?" With a nonchalance that almost infuriated her, he checked his watch and offered a fake scowl. "Ah, I'm sorry. I guess I am a few minutes early."

The time wasn't the problem. The problem was his very presence. He was so handsome, so perfectly charming, and so thoroughly impossible. Mr. Barnett's conversation from earlier still rang in her ears. *When life offers you an opportunity, you should take it.* But what was she supposed to do when the opportunity wasn't hers to take? When she couldn't possibly let herself feel for someone because they weren't meant to be together?

Gripping the strap of her bag currently slung over her shoulder, she shifted her weight from one foot to the other.

"It's just I wasn't expecting you to be so—"

"Devilishly handsome?"

"I don't know. I just wasn't expecting you to be so *here*. I thought we were meeting at your hotel."

Cole strode a little closer, fully comfortable with this situation despite the fact that Rose couldn't have been *less* comfortable.

"Well, I happened to watch a little movie called *It Happened One Night* again, and I think it's bad manners to let a lady go out unescorted. Who knows what kind of ne'er-do-wells could be lurking out here in the shadows? May I?"

In a grand, sweeping gesture, he offered her his arm. Not for the first time, she wondered why in the world he needed chemistry lessons. This man could have chemistry with a fence post. Rose tossed back her shoulders in an attempt to loosen them. They were friends. Two friends. Having fun. No need to assume the worst of him and think he was doing something as ridiculous as *flirting* with her.

"Sure," she said, slipping her arm into his. Together, they started off down the street. "But just so you know, I didn't have escorting single ladies in our lesson plan. It's a little bit old-fashioned."

"Yes, I remember your very intensive course curriculum, but we do have a reputation to uphold now. I'd hate for anyone in town to think I wasn't treating you well."

"Where are you leading me? My car isn't back here, you know. I park down the street."

Strangely enough, he hadn't led her down the front street, the one lining the square, but instead, had taken her back around the other side of the tidy row of buildings, through a back alley illuminated by work lamps. She recognized this street; it was where Harper brought in her weekly delivery of flowers from the farm.

"Well, tonight is supposed to be lesson one, right? Shared experience? I took the liberty of finding something for us to try."

When he pulled them to a stop in front of an otherwise non-descript, grey door painted with the image of a single slice of pie, though, Rose felt her stomach tighten. "What is this?"

"Rose Anderson, welcome to Millie's Pie Joint."

The door to the back kitchen of Millie's swung open, immediately assaulting Rose with the scents of butter and sugar and fresh berries and the sight of bright, streaming golden light from within. The entire picture—Cole standing there, beckoning her to follow him into her favorite place in the world, trading on the idea that they would spend time there together like a real couple would—set her on edge. It was *too* perfect, too romantic, and it awakened a whole host of forbidden feelings deep inside of her.

They needed to get out of here. And fast.

"I know where we are, but I already had a lesson in mind, and it didn't include pie."

"And what was your lesson?"

"I thought we might go fishing."

Cole's eyes were dancing now, shining with unspent laughter.

"At the Miller's Pond? The one with the skinny-dipping?"

"There's too much moon now. There wouldn't be any skinny-dipping when it's so bright out," Rose word-vomited, quick as she could.

But Cole wasn't accepting any of her distractions. Instead of acquiescing and following her out to her truck, where she'd stored the fishing supplies for a long evening of conversation and bait and moonlight—a very tame, very non-romantic activity—he fished around in the pocket of his jacket for something.

"Well, believe it or not, I prefer pie to fish. And the manager here is a big fan of my work. So she gave me…" Finally, he found what he'd been looking for, and flashed a piece of paper written with curving handwriting in her direction. Rose felt herself go sheet-white at the sight of it. "This."

"That cannot be what I think it is."

"Your eyes don't deceive you. Millie's secret blackberry bramble pie recipe, passed down through the years and, finally, into your waiting hands."

He offered it to her. Rose's vision tunneled around it. No one, not even the best investigative journalists at the *Hillsboro Gazette* had been able to get that secret recipe. It was a family secret, one that the Talleys had sworn to take with them to their graves.

And Cole had gotten it. Just for her. Just because he knew that she liked it.

"I can't take that."

"Why not?"

"Because it's the most secret recipe in the entire world! I'll just screw it up. I'm a terrible cook! I'll besmirch the name of Millie's Pie Joint and never forgive myself."

As he spoke, he reached onto the counter and pulled a handful of fabric away with him. As he looped it over his head, she realized it was an apron. "Rose, sometimes, you've got to take a chance. That's what your novels have been telling me, at least. Besides, what's a better shared experience than making a pie?"

"Even if it's terrible, it will be a good memory."

"Exactly. Now, how do I look?" He struck a pose. Typical movie star. "I really think pink is my color."

"Come on. *Every* color is your color," Rose snarked, tying her own apron and trying not to think about just how kissable and handsome he was. "Is that a movie star thing? Do they teach you how to look good in everything? Or is that something you learned from your family? Maybe your dad is a model or something?"

She began to inspect the recipe card he'd given her, comparing it to the bowls and ingredients measured out in front of them. They would need to work fast to make the pie crust—the recipe was very specific about cutting cold butter into the mixture.

When he didn't answer her question, she glanced up at him from over the index card. He blinked too fast. His left hand balled into a fist. His eyes were distant.

"Cole?" she asked.

He crashed back down to earth. "No, not my family. My dad wasn't anybody special. Guess I was just lucky."

Something about that answer didn't sit well with her. Not wrong, exactly, just…not right. She pressed: "You've met my embarrassing family. Come on, you can tell me a little bit about yours. What are they like?"

"Oh, you don't want to hear about my family. Besides, you're not one to talk."

"About what?"

"About looking good in everything."

Her heart fluttered. She tried to focus on the butter and the flour. If he'd wanted to bail out of the family conversation, he'd succeeded in distracting her.

"Are you trying out new lines for your script? I read some of the pages. The romantic dialogue is…"

"Yeah," he winced. "It can be a little rough at times. Would that be okay? If I tried out some new lines on you?"

Yes. No. Only if you mean them. Only if you don't. Rose lifted a small smile.

"Maybe we should make this pie first. Romantic movie lines later."

"Aye, chef."

An hour and a half later, they both slid pieces of a slightly wonky-looking pie onto matching plates. Cheeks aching from laughter, Rose could feel that most of her face was still covered in flour and streaks of blueberry juice, but considering that Cole was sporting matching stains, she decided she didn't care so much. Besides, this was the moment of truth. To see if the secret recipe they'd been given was *actually* Millie's, and to see if they had followed it correctly.

Three, two, one. Rose scooped a bite onto her fork and then into her mouth, where the sweet, tangy, buttery, acidic mix of fruits, starches and sweets danced together on her tongue, warming her from the inside out.

It was perfect. Absolutely perfect.

Her mother always said that things tasted better when they were made with love—that's what she'd told Harper, anyway, any time she bemoaned the fact that she couldn't cook or bake anything to save her life—and when Rose opened her eyes after moaning into the perfect bite of pie, her gaze settled on Cole and that phrase came to mind.

She shook her head to clear it. She didn't love Cole. They'd just made a good pie together, that was all.

"Okay," Cole said, his friendly, casual grin a little wider and brighter than usual. He spoke through a mouthful of pie. "I'm not going to say that we're putting Millie out of business—"

"You'd better not say that!"

"But I really do think that if we opened up across the street, making nothing but this, they'd be shuttering this place in no time."

Rose tossed back her head in a laugh. It *was* delicious, but she'd be leaving the pie making to Millie's baking team from now on. They were the experts, and her arms were already sore from all of the dough rolling they'd had to do with the pie crust.

"I've got to hand it to you, Cole. I *am* really impressed. Somehow, you managed to help the worst baker in the family make something halfway edible."

"See? You and I make a good team."

Don't read too much into that. Don't let yourself enjoy this too much, Rose reminded herself, as harshly as she could. But even as she tried to drag herself back to reality—the reality where they lived, the one where she and Cole could never be together—she found herself smiling and agreeing with him.

"Fine. You were right. The pie making was way more fun than the fishing would have been. But one of these days, I'm going to get you out to that pond."

"Rose! If you want me to go skinny-dipping, all you have to do is ask!"

That particular comment, she only answered by flinging a spoonful of whipped cream in his face. He deserved it.

And, he looked surprisingly cute with a streak of whipped cream across his lips. A fact she tried not to dwell on.

"Can I ask you a question?" she asked, her eyes flickering down to those lips despite her best efforts.

"Yeah, sure," he said.

"This was really nice."

"Not a question."

She shoved her elbow into his side. "I wasn't finished yet."

"Ah, of course," he replied in a mockingly serious tone. "Please. Proceed."

"If you're this good at dating, why isn't Vivienne back with you already? I mean, don't get me wrong, having Millie's secret pie recipe is great and all, but…Why don't you just do this kind of stuff for her?"

"You already asked me that. Or something like it."

"Yeah, but now I'm asking it with a generations-old secret pie recipe in my hands."

In the industrial kitchen, the standing dishwasher and the air-filtering unit hummed.

"She isn't the romantic type. She doesn't go for this kind of stuff."

"That's a shame."

"Why?"

"There aren't enough romantics in the world. I'm sorry she'll miss out on you."

Chapter Twelve

Cole

A handful of days and twice as many books passed. Cole's life became a sea of events in which Rose Anderson was the main star.

She was a good tutor. That's what he told himself. And they were friends. Being friends was a perfectly reasonable thing to do, and certainly didn't mean that he was losing sight of his true goal: getting Vivienne and his career back on track.

Cole hadn't had a ton of female friends in his life, so he could only assume it was normal to want to kiss them. Or brush their hair back over their ear. Or want them to finally show you the Miller's Pond, where apparently skinny-dipping went on every time the moon waned enough to give the swimmers a little bit of privacy.

Yes, all very normal, very cool things that happened to two friends. Absolutely.

On the morning of a "secret event" that Rose had planned for them, Cole was busy getting dressed to her specifications—wear clothes you don't mind getting wet and bring an extra pair of clothes to change into later, if the need arises—when his cell phone rang. His management team ensured that his number changed every few weeks, and that only a handful of people had access to that number. It was a safety thing. So, when he picked it up and didn't instantly recognize the number, he went into defensive, uncertain mode.

"Hello?"

"Cole? You changed your number. You wound me."

You wound me. Only one person in the world still spoke like a vixen from an eighties thriller, and it was his ex-girlfriend. Cole's body, which had been on edge when he answered the phone, now practically danced on the edge of a cliff. The hairs on the back of his neck raised and his throat closed, making normal, human speech practically impossible.

How had she gotten this number? Why was she calling him? What did she want? Why was she talking like their last conversation hadn't completely shattered his soul?

And why, at the sound of her voice, did his mind immediately flash, quite guiltily, to thoughts of Rose Anderson?

Cole straightened his spine and tried to offer a coherent response despite all that was silently going on in his head.

"Vivienne. Hi, Vivienne. It's…it's good to hear from you."

"That's the best you can do? Come on, Cole. You used to be so romantic."

Cole's stomach rolled, but he tried to play it off with a good-natured laugh, as if her reactions to his more romantic side had been just an inside joke between lovers instead of part of what had crushed his spirit.

"You were the one who told me that you…What was it? Detest sentimentality?"

"You know the old expression, don't you? You don't know what you've got until it's gone."

She must have *really* missed him, then. Cole sank onto the nearest chair, not trusting his knees to hold him up any longer. He and Vivienne's relationship had been…complicated, to say the least. And it had certainly been complicated by the way she'd ended things and the fact that their entire relationship—beginning, middle, and bitter end—played out in the blistering spotlight. But one thing that had always caused friction between them was the fact that he thought if you were in love with someone, you needed to show them that. She, on the other hand, hated breakfast in bed and handwritten notes left in the fridge or small gestures that let her know he was thinking of her.

To Vivienne, if it wasn't Cartier or a cover story, she didn't want it.

Cole cleared his throat and tried to clear his mind of sour memories. Why was he thinking this way when all he'd wanted for the last few months was to get back with her? Sure, Vivienne had her flaws and sure their relationship wasn't perfect, but that was just life, wasn't it?

"Is there something I can do for you?"

"Why?" Vivienne asked, her voice quick and eager. "Are you in a rush to get out and explore the backwater they've sent you to? Lots of appointments to keep at the local corn maze and watering hole?"

"They mostly do wine and flowers up here, actually."

"Sounds beautiful," she said, though Cole doubted her sincerity.

"It is."

Crackling cell phone silence. If she was waiting for Cole to say something, she'd be waiting a long time. He was properly tongue-tied. He was talking to Vivienne. Talking to the woman he'd been wanting to get back with since the moment they broke up. And he didn't have a single thing to say to her.

He flashed back to the conversations he'd had with Rose about this woman. He held her up as a symbol of everything he'd ever wanted from his career in Hollywood. She was successful. She was seen. She was known. But Rose didn't see it that way. Rose saw her as disappointing, as someone who didn't see him for who he truly was.

Now, listening to her on the phone, the creeping sense that he might have been wrong while Rose might have been right wrapped its cold hand around the back of his neck.

"You know, I was thinking, actually," Vivienne purred, apparently unruffled by his silence. "L.A. has become such an absolute *bore* recently. But you seem to be having a very…productive time up in your little town. What is it called again?"

"Hillsboro."

"Hillsboro," she repeated. "Well, I thought that maybe I could come up and have a visit. Get some fresh air. Drink the wine and smell the roses."

Cole's heart pounded. Had she meant to bring Rose into this conversation?

Had she been reading the papers and getting the scoop on his relationship? Had his plan to make her jealous kind of, almost, sort of worked? And if it had…why didn't he feel better about it?

With his free hand rising to rub the back of his neck self-consciously, Cole tried to play both sides towards the middle, trying to gauge her better.

"You don't really like small towns," he angled, trying his best to lure her out. "You always said that the city is where you feel most at home."

"And it is! But everyone needs a change of pace sometimes."

Heat flared up inside of him again. He'd tried to give her a change of pace several times, and every time he did, she came up with some excuse for why she *simply couldn't*. She was allergic to grass. The sun didn't suit her. She wouldn't be able to leave her apartment for an entire weekend. Small towns gave her the creeps.

It's a shame. There aren't enough romantics in the world. That's what Rose had said.

"I tried to take you on a trip to Martha's Vineyard and you said—"

"Cole," she snapped, her voice a sharp and potent reminder of their last argument. But just as soon as his defenses rose, they fell when her voice lowered back into its sweet, dulcet purrs. He could almost see her lips pouting as she spoke. "I'm beginning to get the feeling that you don't *want* to see me. But that couldn't be right. Could it?"

"No! I'd love to see you. And Hillsboro is great. It's really great."

Again, there was Rose. Right in the forefront of his mind. With her easy smile and the way she pressed her glasses up the bridge of her nose, the way she always made him feel like a person instead of a collection of talents and "starring" credits and the way she melted a little bit whenever he smiled at her and the way she challenged him and made him laugh and—

"Well," Vivienne replied, after a moment of hesitation, "I don't have any firm plans yet, but I think it would be nice to get together when I'm in town. I don't like the way we left things."

That was the first time she'd even acknowledged their breakup to him. Everything else she thought about it, he'd heard through the tabloids. All of the stitched-up wounds he thought he'd been healing suddenly ripped wide open. Breath momentarily became very difficult to find. "I…I'd like that, too."

"Okay, then. I've got to go. But it was so good hearing your voice. See you soon, Cole."

Before he could answer her, the dial tone erupted from the other end of the phone. He muttered into the static. "Yeah. See you soon."

Rose made good on her promise to eventually get him out fishing. She hadn't brought him to the Miller's Pond—probably to avoid any more of his skinny-dipping jokes—but to a place out on her family's property called Sae's. A little creek that cut through the forest and ran out to the town's lake beyond. Despite the fact that this was supposed to be some kind of lesson in shared experience and chemistry, this was quieter than their last date had been. Cole would have liked to think that the quiet was natural, an extension of the calm, rippling waters and the playful game of tag that the wind was playing through the trees. He would have liked to believe that his own unnatural quiet came from the peace of this place, that it was settling the chaos in his bones and making him one with the land or something.

But he knew better. He was thinking about Vivienne and their phone call this afternoon. He was thinking about Rose Anderson and the way her braided pigtails and overalls made her look like the most kissable pin-up model he'd ever seen. He was thinking about how the small fork in the stream up ahead reminded him of his own life.

In one direction, there was Vivienne. In the other, there was Rose. He knew Rose wasn't for him. She'd made it clear that she didn't want any romantic entanglements and she didn't want any complications in her life, and he respected that. He needed to keep his focus on Vivienne. Hadn't that call been everything he'd been waiting for since the moment she walked out of his life?

If it was, why couldn't he stop thinking about Rose?

"Alright," Rose deadpanned, her voice rising up against the smooth waters of the creek. "Something's wrong with you."

"Something's wrong with me? You're the one who's barely touched the snacks."

She'd brought a picnic basket full of small-town treats to the creek with her, but today marked the first time he'd ever seen Rose Anderson and sweets in the same vicinity without her immediately inhaling them. As she adjusted the reel in her hands, she shrugged with a half-smirk.

"I'm not touching my pie because by now, I'm used to you stealing bites. I'm trying to leave you enough to steal."

Silence resumed again. Well, not quite silence. There was the giggle of the water and the humming of the bugs and the distant barking of the family dog, Stella. And the echoing of his own thoughts, which seemed to get louder the quieter everything else grew.

"Can I ask you a question?"

"Oh, here we go."

"What?" Cole asked.

"You should have learned by now. Every time someone in a romance novel or a romcom says, 'Can I ask you a question?' it turns the whole conversation serious and boring."

Once again, she adjusted her reel, and Cole tried to copy her motions. He wasn't exactly the fishing type. Neither of them had gotten a bite all day. He shook his head and tried to laugh.

"I just want some advice."

"I'm not so good at the advice thing, remember? That's why everyone feels entitled to dole it out to me all the time."

With the big, white shrimping boots Rose had lent him from her father's collection, Cole edged closer to her place in the water. He couldn't help but admire the way she stood in the center of the busy stream—a calm, certain, still being, unmoved by the rushing around her. He envied her a little bit, too.

"Why haven't you found someone already, Rose? What are you hiding from?"

She stilled, and tried to shrug off his question. The words fell off of her tongue easily, but there was a slight bite to the end of them. "Not much. Why? Is that what you really want to know? My tragic backstory?"

He didn't like the sound of the word tragic, not when it came from her lips. But he wanted to understand why. Why someone who cherished romance and love was hiding herself from both.

"Shared story is one of the four pillars of chemistry, isn't it?"

"That's not on the lesson plan for a few more days yet," she reminded him, never taking her eyes off of the waters ahead of her.

"Come on," Cole said, his fishing pole practically forgotten in his hands. "Surely you know you can trust me by now."

Rose didn't look his way, not at first, anyway. She searched the stream as though it would have answers, then at him as if he had any. When she realized they were all just as helpless and clueless as each other, she drank in a sigh and offered the beginning of her story.

"When I was younger, I couldn't find a good guy to save my life. All through high school, I thought, you know, on the first day of school, every year, I would show up and think to myself, this is the year. This is the year that some cool, sensitive loner transfers in from out of state, and he becomes my one true love. And then I went to college and thought that a bigger dating pool might help me find someone, but—"

"That didn't work out either."

Something in his gut twisted. Rose Anderson was the kindest, warmest, most complicated and lovely woman he'd ever met. The fact that she'd gone through her entire life without anyone having shown her that made him slightly sick.

"Exactly. So, anyway, I started the whole online dating thing. I know, I should have known better, but I didn't."

"I know lots of people who have found love online," Cole offered, trying to be judicious, trying not to make her feel any worse about herself than she already did. Of all the sins one could commit, trying online dating seemed like the least of them.

"And I was swayed by the commercials that promised me a perfect love story like that. I got totally taken in. And, eventually this guy popped up. Luka. Handsome as all get out. Charming. Funny. He told me he lived in San Francisco, but was thinking of moving to Hillsboro after getting burned out in the tech world."

"But he wasn't?"

"You already know this story doesn't have a happy ending," Rose said, glancing at him with a teasing smile that didn't quite meet her eyes. "You don't get any points for guessing."

"Sorry. Go on."

Reeling in her line so she could recast, Rose continued, her voice getting darker in tone and thicker with each word, as if they were getting stuck in her throat the longer she talked. She tried to play it all off with a self-deprecating grin, but he knew better by now. It was Rose's way, to try and hide the ugliness in her life. After all, it *was* her life, and she got to decide how people saw it. But that smile of hers couldn't take the edge off of this story any more than a touch of concealer could have covered up a black eye.

"Well, it turned out his name wasn't Luka. One day, this girl shows up at my shop, and she tells me the truth. Or what she thought was the truth. He wasn't a handsome, funny, charismatic man who could make me laugh and feel like no one else could. She said he was a sociopathic computer nerd living in Tampa, lying about who he really was to lure in all of these women. Hundreds of them."

A pause. Cole waited it out.

"And I told her she was crazy. That she was lying. That she didn't know him like I did. I mean, he'd *promised* he was going to move to the Bay Area. We'd talked for hours and hours about him helping me start my own perfume company. We were going to have a life together."

At the end of that sentence, Rose's voice broke. She cleared her throat before she could continue.

"So, she gave me his address. And I was so sure I was going to prove her wrong that I emptied out my savings, told my family that I was going to a conference, and went there. But she was right. He was doing the same thing to almost a hundred girls. Using some other guy's pictures and videos to convince us he was real. He even had a spreadsheet of all of us, so he could make sure he kept us all straight and didn't confuse our relationships. He showed me. He was *proud* of it. And when I told him that he was a monster, he laughed in my face and told me that if he was a monster, then that made me a delusional little princess."

Cole wasn't deep enough in the water to feel seasick, but that's what he was. "Rose, that's disgusting. You didn't deserve that."

"I know," she said, the confidence slowly creeping back into her voice. "But ever since then, I've had a hard time trusting people. No, really, I've had a hard time trusting myself. As soon as I found out what was going on, all of the obvious lies in his story started showing through. How could I have been so blind? So stupid? And if I could get fooled by someone that horrible into giving away my heart, who's to say it wouldn't happen again?"

"So, to protect yourself, you've just stopped trusting anyone? In case you fall for a bad guy again?"

She nodded, once. Cole had been hoping that she'd tell him about her life and he'd come away with some kind of North Star that would point him right back in Vivienne's direction. He'd hoped Rose would look at him and say, "Don't give up on love, it's the most precious thing in the world. I wish I'd never given up my great love story," or something sappy and over-the-top like that. But that wasn't the case. Instead, he was more conflicted than ever.

Maybe…Maybe Vivienne wasn't all he'd remembered her to be. Maybe she wasn't right for him. And, in any case, Rose wasn't off-limits to him because she *really* believed that love would find her in its own time and in its own way. Rose was hiding because she didn't want to get hurt again.

"That's the gist of it, yep. I think people can do a lot of desperate things if it means that they won't get screwed over again. This is just what I do."

Another light bulb went off in the back of Cole's mind.

"And *that's* why you don't want to lie to your family. You don't want to be like that guy."

"Man, you really are good at this psychoanalysis, aren't you?" she teased. "Or am I really that easy to read?"

"No, you're not easy to read at all. But that's one of the things that I love about being with you, Rose. You're a mystery in so many ways."

Rose went quiet then. She reeled in her hook again. Nothing was biting. "I'm not sure anyone else sees me like that."

"Maybe they aren't looking the way that I do."

Chapter Thirteen

Rose

In her workshop—the Smell Shack, as her sister called it—Rose couldn't help but contemplate what she'd done when she confessed the truth to Cole. Only two people in the entire world knew about her short-lived, whirlwind disaster of a relationship with the catfishing account formerly known as Luka. Herself, and Annie Martin, who she'd told when Annie's own relationship with George—her current boyfriend—had been on the rocks. And now, apparently, so did Cole.

At first, she wasn't sure why she'd told him. It had been one of her life's biggest secrets, one she hadn't even shared with her sisters or her parents. For years, it had been a private shame. A trauma she dealt with by shoving it down into a little lockbox buried somewhere in the depths of her heart.

Luka had lied to her about *everything*. He'd made her believe in a person and in a love that didn't exist. She'd pinned her hopes, her dreams and her future on those lies, and the shame of that had forced her to stay as quiet about it as she possibly could. She still felt he'd tainted them. He'd laughed behind her back at the idea she could ever be successful. Confessing that to someone else…it was humiliating.

But when Cole had asked her, she'd just…told him. Fishing pole in hand, she'd stared out at the cool waters of the stream and repeated the sad facts of her life.

And he'd accepted her. Been kind to her. Told her that she didn't deserve it. All of the things she hadn't been able to make herself believe, especially from someone who barely knew her.

Only, that wasn't true either, was it? With all of the talking they'd been doing lately, it seemed that maybe he knew her better than just about anybody.

The only people who claimed to know her better? Harper Anderson and Annie Martin, who were currently trying not to make too much noise right outside of her workshop. For a while, Rose did a valiant job of ignoring them. After all, they'd been meddling in her life for too long. She wasn't in the mood for more of that today. But when a knock came on the door, avoiding them proved an impossible dream.

"Rose?"

"Come in. Oh, hi, you two," she said, pretending to be too busy to pay them much attention when, in reality, she wasn't doing much more than reorganizing her essences collection.

"Rose, we wanted to talk to you," Annie blurted out, an approach that apparently hadn't been planned, at least if Harper's annoyed grunt was to be believed.

"Why?" Rose asked, idly.

Harper spoke next. "We wanted to apologize. Annie for the reporter thing. Me for all the romance talk."

A laugh choked from her throat as she set a handful of empty, colorful jars in the window over her small mixing sink. The light caught their bellies, casting stained-glass glows across Rose's skin. "What, you aren't going to send poor Mr. Barnett to do it for you? Hm, Annie?"

"No," Annie grumbled. "Obviously that didn't work and I don't pursue losing strategies."

"Annie!" Harper snapped.

"I'm joking! Look, Rose knows I'm joking."

"We wanted to apologize," Rose's sister snapped, trying to clear the air as quickly and effectively as she could. "And we wanted to make it up to you. We've got wine and junk food and comfy PJs."

The offer was tempting. Rose couldn't remember the last time she'd gone this long without a girls' night with at least one of her sisters or Annie. She loved those nights, loved spending time with the people she cared most about in this world. Still, she couldn't help but keep her walls high as she wiped down the already clean counters of her workstation.

"Do either of you even know what you're saying sorry for? Or are you just tired of me not being around to clean up your messes?"

Harsh words. She could practically feel Harper flinch behind her.

"No," she said. "We know what we did wrong. We weren't fair to you or to your feelings. And we're sorry."

"Yeah, we're really sorry. We just—"

Rose cut Annie off before she could say the words that Rose had come to hate more than any other in the English language. "Want me to be happy. I know."

"And we thought," Annie said, her voice lifting up a little to its normal, cheery pitch, "that we could start making you happy on your terms with a pie and taco night...? If you're interested and not seeing Cole tonight, of course."

"Cole and I had breakfast at his hotel this morning before we went fishing. We've fulfilled our hanging out obligation for the day," Rose said, noncommittally.

The truth was, a pie and tacos and pajamas night sounded good. Better than good. Just what she needed to get her mind off of baking at Millie's with Cole or how she'd laughed until her sides hurt this morning as Cole explained to her the "Official Cole McKittrick Hierarchy of Breakfast Buffet Bagels."

"Good, because we really got *way* too many tacos. There's no way we could finish them all without you."

Well, in that case, Rose knew she couldn't refuse. It would be a crime to let perfectly good tacos (and a perfectly good apology) go to waste. Ten minutes later, they were snuggled up on the couch, ready for a night of binge-watching and snacking to their hearts' content. Rose found herself slipping back into the easy rhythm. Some people thought it was weird that she, at her age, was still living on the same property as her parents. But the attic was basically her own apartment, and with the investments she put into her shop every year...well, living with her parents for a few more months was worth it to get to do what she loved. Tonight, her parents were blissfully away at a music festival, meaning that Rose, Annie, and Harper had the entire place to themselves.

Which was good, because if their mom had heard the way Annie was talking about Rose and Cole, she might have passed out cold on the kitchen tiles.

"So…will you tell us a little bit about how things are going with Cole?"

"I'm sure you saw the papers and have heard the rumors around town," Rose said, trying not to put lying labels on everything. "You can put the pieces together, I bet. You're both pretty smart."

"Yeah, but we want to hear it from you," Harper said, sliding up to the kitchen counter and taking a seat at one of the high barstools as Rose selected her first plate of tacos.

"Cole and I are just hanging out. It would be impossible between us anyway."

"You're not hanging out. You're dating. Come on. We can all see that. And that's what's giving me pause here, Rose," Harper intoned. "You *never* do anything if you're not sure it'll last forever. That's just the kind of person you are. So, he has to be special."

"Did you guys just apologize to me about interfering in my love life so you could ask about my love life? Seriously?"

With a flick of an annoyed wrist, Rose almost sent the spicy shrimp taco in her hands flying across the kitchen.

"No!" Annie piped up. "We can totally talk about other things."

"Such as?"

"Such as…" Clearly, she hadn't given much thought to what she might say before declaring that they could *totally* talk about things that weren't romance, but it took a full moment of *ummm* for Annie to finally come up with her answer. "Such as: have you given any more thought to my proposal?"

"Your ridiculous perfume idea?" Rose scoffed.

"Yes! Your stuff is amazing. You've got to get it out there. Just put a few vials in May's shop, let that sweet Tina girl who's running it now give people the hard sell, and I promise that once people start wearing it, you'll be able to leave your little flower shop for good and start doing the perfume thing full-time."

Ah, yes. Yet another one of the things in life—like love—that Rose really wanted, but couldn't let herself have. Starting her own perfume brand and going global—all of that big dream stuff…she'd given that up after the whole Luka incident. It was too terrifying. No, she loved her flower shop, she loved doing flower arrangements. Maybe she loved getting to work on her perfumes *more*, but it was safer to keep it as a hobby. That would have to be enough.

"I like my little flower shop," Rose mumbled.

"Right, but you could be the next Jo Malone. Or the next…the next…" It was clear that, while Annie knew plenty about fashion designers and wellness brands, her knowledge of famous perfumers was surprisingly limited. "Well, you could be the *first* Rose Anderson, and that is all that matters. Besides, who wouldn't want to buy a perfume by someone named Rose? It's perfect. And you might finally have enough money to move out of your family's loft."

"I'm perfectly happy making my perfume just for fun and giving it out to friends. Making scents that are perfect for someone is a really nice, relaxing thing for me. I don't need to monetize my hobbies. Besides, I'm going to get out of the loft very soon. Don't you worry. I've been saving up for my own place."

Very soon was relative. By Rose's estimation, she wouldn't be out of her family's house for another six months or so, but still. After living in one place for twenty-eight years, six months would be nothing.

"So," Harper asked, eyebrows fully waggling now. "Did you make one for Cole yet?"

"I thought we'd talked about avoiding my love life in this particular conversation."

"We did, but I am *way* too curious. Sorry."

She probably should have been expecting this question. After all, that was what Rose did when she liked someone—as a friend, a colleague or a family member. She took everything she knew about them, from their personalities to their likes to the stories they'd told her, and distilled all of that down into a bottle until she had the essence of that person, a perfume she could give them when the time was right.

But making someone a perfume was special for Rose. It was a sign that she cared about them more deeply than she had any right to care about Cole. It usually took her days just to think of what notes she wanted to include in the scent, much less to make the darn thing. That would be simply too much time to dedicate to her fake boyfriend, despite the fact that the scents were already floating around in her head, waiting to be bottled.

"No, I haven't made one for Cole."

"Why not? He'd be the perfect candidate," Harper said, through a mouth full of carne asada.

Rose snorted. At least for this, she had an answer that didn't force her to lie. "It's a bit weird to be like, 'Hey, I know we've only been seeing each other for a week, but here, I made a *perfume* for you.'"

"He's a celebrity. He's probably had weirder encounters."

"I want to be his friend. Not his fan."

Strange. She and Cole had never actually talked about his stardom or his celebrity status. Their conversations were more personal than that. Making a mental note to ask him about it the next time she saw him, she tucked the thought away for later examination.

"I get the feeling you want to be *way more* than his friend, though. Can you tell us if he's a good kisser?"

"This conversation is *so* over!" Rose snapped, but with a smile.

"You're right," Harper said, trying to play peacemaker. "Time for pie and binge-watching some old nineties show until our eyes fall out."

"And it wouldn't be a sleepover without wine," Annie announced, rushing to the fridge to snap up a chilled bottle of pale pink rosé with the local Barn Door Winery's label on the front.

"None for me, thanks. I'm done with making bad, wine-induced decisions for a lifetime."

What if she had a little too much to drink again and did something stupid, like call her fake, totally not real boyfriend and ask him if he was serious about all the nice things he said to her? If the butterflies she sometimes got when he peered in her direction were only flutterings in her stomach.

"I don't know. Last time you got tipsy, you thoroughly charmed one Mr. Cole McKittrick, so much so that in eight days since you met him, you've seen him eight times."

"Harper," Rose asked, glaring at her sister across the tabletop and pointing to their sweet, but mouthy friend. "Will you get this girl a piece of pie?"

"Coming right up."

"She needs something other than my romantic life to keep her mouth busy."

Hours later, when the pie tin was almost empty and they'd reached what felt like their thousandth episode of *Sabrina the Teenage Witch* (the original, of course), Rose found her mind wandering. While it was nice to be with Annie and Harper again, and while she felt comfortable and at peace in their presence now that they'd mostly cleared the air between them, there was still one thing that she couldn't shake, one feeling that dominated all of the others. Uncertainty.

Harper and Annie were two of the most stubborn people she'd ever met, and she lived in a small town where people felt that obstinacy was a virtue on par with patience, so that was really saying something. They wouldn't have just woken up one day and decided to reconcile with her. It wasn't in their nature. Which meant that there had to be some kind of outside force pushing them in her direction. But where that outside force had come from, Rose couldn't even begin to guess. Her mother wasn't one to meddle in that way. Her father had been carefully keeping his distance ever since he'd caught Rose using the company shredder to get rid of all the copies of the paparazzi pictures of her and Cole. That didn't leave a lot of options.

"Can I ask you something, Harper?" Rose asked, glancing at her sister in the glow of the television set. Annie had fallen into a deep sugar coma after her third slice of pie, leaving Harper and Rose alone to chat in whispers.

"Yeah?" Harper replied.

"What was with the sudden change of heart? Both of you seemed pretty content to leave me alone."

"We weren't content to leave you alone; we were trying to give you space. We felt like we'd been suffocating you, so we thought you might not react well if we just, you know, pounced and tried to drag you back into our lives."

"Right," Rose agreed, seeing that line of logic but not knowing how it led them here. "So, what changed? Why did you suddenly decide to apologize?"

The living room was dim, but the couch cushions rustled as Harper silently squirmed for a too-long moment. "Well…" She drank in a deep sigh, then spoke. "Cole came and saw us last night."

Rose's heart thudded. *No. Please. Anything but that.*

"He did *what?*"

"He saw us having dinner near his hotel and he reminded us that we weren't being very good to you. That it wasn't fair to stay away and lick our wounds when you were the one hurting."

Heat flared up at the back of Rose's neck. Of all the people she thought would understand. No, Cole was the only one who *could* understand. The only one who she'd been completely honest with about all her feelings. He knew how she felt about other people trying to invade her life. Yet he'd done exactly what everyone else thought they had the freedom to do in her life. He meddled.

"So, he told you to come and apologize to me?"

"No, he pointed out we'd hurt you. That this wasn't just like a normal sister fight. And that we were in the wrong and needed to make things right."

It wasn't the worst betrayal Rose had ever felt in her life, but still, it stung. She'd thought that she and Cole understood each other, that for the first time in a long time, she'd found someone who actually saw her not as the simple, unassuming person she'd pretended to be, but as the complicated, mixed-up person she really was on the inside.

She was wrong. She was also, for a long moment, completely silent.

"Rose?" Harper eventually prompted. "Rose, are you okay?"

"Yeah. I'm fine." Everything in her body told her the exact opposite. Her jaw tensed. Her stomach rioted. Her nostrils flared and the tips of her ears went so hot she wondered if she had spontaneously started running a fever. Then, in an instant, she went completely numb. Cold. "I just can't believe no one trusts me to take care of myself. It's ridiculous."

"That's not how it felt—"

"Yeah, maybe not to *you*. But how do you think it feels to me that my sister and my best friend don't think that they need to apologize to me until some big, strong man sweeps in and makes them?"

This was the problem with letting her feelings out, with being honest with herself about how everyone else's treatment of her made her feel. Now that she'd started, she couldn't stop.

"We're really sorry, Rose," came the soft, whispered, repentant reply.

"Yeah. I know you are. And so am I."

Sorry she thought she could ever trust anyone. Especially Cole McKittrick.

Chapter Fourteen

Cole

It had been over a week since his move to Hillsboro and Cole found it strange how easily he'd adapted to small-town living. Well, easily wasn't the right word. He still missed the big city and all of its particular charm, but…there was something about the people here that fascinated him. They were genuinely good people who looked out for each other, who had each other's backs, who worked together to build the kind of flourishing, diverse, beautiful community they wanted.

A community that now, apparently, included him.

After his Hollywood shine had worn off, no one gave him a second look when he ducked into the coffee shop for a cup or sat in the park with a baseball cap on to study his lines, as he was now. In fact, once or twice, he was sure he'd actually heard a local dissuade a tourist when they'd suggested that it was *the* Cole McKittrick sitting in their midst. "That guy? Oh, no, that's just Bill. But he gets that a lot. Go on over and ask for his autograph. He'll get a kick out of it."

Inevitably, the tourist would move on before bothering Cole for that autograph, not wanting to embarrass themselves, meaning that (for the most part) Cole's life proved relatively undisturbed out here. Even the tabloid press kept surprisingly out of sight and out of mind once Annie was done giving them tips on where he would be and when he'd make it there.

But that was the trouble. It was like, when he was here, he wasn't a celebrity. Did he miss the fans harassing him at every corner, like they did in Los Angeles? No. Did he miss having to hide his face every time he went to the grocery store? No, of course not. But celebrity did help him achieve certain goals.

Goals like not having to answer frantic, panicked calls from his agent every half-hour, where he was pitched ridiculous ideas of how to boost his profile even while out here in the sticks. Celebrity meant he was too busy for taking those calls. Goals like making Vivienne jealous with all of the press and publicity he was getting. Celebrity meant the cameras were usually interested in him, and were more than happy to meddle in his relationships.

Once again, he found himself sitting on a bench near the calm, musical hum of the water feature in the center of the town square, waiting for Rose to finish her shift at work so they could have another one of their lessons. The lessons had been helpful as he went about learning his lines and studying up for when production would kick off next week. He'd spent hours, often late into the night, marking his scripts with all he had learned about romance and inner torment and what falling in love really felt and looked like. But really, his mind kept wandering back to Vivienne and the conversation he and Rose had by the creek. This entire scheme of his hadn't really been about the lessons, not when he got down to it. It'd had been about making Vivienne jealous.

Now, he had a choice to make. What was his priority? Vivienne would be coming to Hillsboro any day now. What would he do when she got there? Would he turn his back on Rose and their agreement at the first sign that Vivienne wanted him back? Or would he stand by Rose as they'd agreed, and see their partnership through until he went back to Los Angeles?

What did he *really* want?

The words on the pages before him blurred the longer he sat there, swimming out of focus the longer he was lost in thought. He needed to be honest with himself, needed to come clean about what his own heart wanted from this situation. But he didn't know how.

"Um, sir?"

Glancing up from his script, Cole tucked a receipt into the pages to serve as a bookmark. In that small moment of quiet he'd bought himself, he affixed his movie-star smile and conjured up as much charm as he could muster. He'd never wanted to be one of those celebrities who grew inflated egos and were rude to strangers just because they could be, and he wasn't about to start now. When he did look up, he met the gaze of a slightly frumpy librarian type in her late sixties, who clutched her sweater around her despite the fact that they were practically bathing in sunshine right now.

"Yes, can I help you?"

"I hate to bother you, but you're seeing Rose Anderson, aren't you?"

Cole only had a split second in which to parse that language and determine whether or not it technically fit the rules he and Rose had laid out for themselves when they'd started this thing. Technically, yes, he saw her every day, so it seemed acceptable.

"I sure am. Has word really gotten around town so fast?"

Yeah, turned out that the charm wasn't necessary. Mrs. Librarian wasn't responsive to it. She swallowed hard, shifting on the balls of her orthopedic shoes.

"Yes, but, I'm sorry, but—there's something going on at the flower shop and I really think you should look into it."

"What?"

Her wrinkles deepened as concern gripped her. "Just go, please!"

That was all the invitation Cole needed. If Rose was in trouble, as this lady seemed to think she was, then he wasn't just going to continue hanging out in the park and ignore the problem. Hell, even if the issue was as simple as Rose needing a box off of a high shelf, he wanted to be there to help her manage it.

As it was, when Cole arrived outside of Rose's shop, script tucked under one arm, what he saw through the window was a definite alert step above boxes on high shelves. His entire body stiffened as he caught the sight of a smoothly manicured, slightly short, but surprisingly muscular man standing in the center of the shop floor. He recognized the man almost instantly, not by his build, which wouldn't have looked out of place in any posers' convention in Los Angeles, but by the ratty, black sweatshirt with red writing that the man always wore when he was at work. The fading lettering read AMERICA'S NEWS across the sweatshirt's front, back, and down both sleeves, warning people from all angles that he worked for the most voracious tabloid out there.

He knew this man well. Terrence Milgreen, the "reporter" who had basically haunted his every move since he'd started working on his show. Cole's heart sped up as he practically threw himself into the shop, just in time to watch Terrence pressing himself against

Rose's counter, encroaching on her personal space as she tried to politely put as much distance between them as the small back work area of her shop allowed. Everything about her screamed discomfort. Cole's instincts roared to life.

Terrence was currently in the middle of a long, stream-of-consciousness ramble of questions, his usual gimmick. "And where did you and Cole meet? When did you meet? Is this an on-location fling or—"

Rose's pink face slackened when she caught sight of him in the doorway. "Cole!"

He didn't have time to register how he felt about Rose feeling safe and reassured in his presence. Instead, he focused his energies on the man currently turning to face him.

"What are you doing here?"

"Hey, look at this! Just the man I wanted to see. The bachelor of the hour." Terrence spoke words like bullets, hot and fast and too quick to catch. A camera hung between his hands, which he used to idly snap pictures of the store, of Rose, of Cole, as he spoke. "Me and your girlfriend here were just chatting. You know, getting to know each other since I've been officially assigned to the Hillsboro beat for the duration of the shoot here. Lots of big names in this movie, huh, Cole?"

"Rose, did you ask this guy to come in here?"

A dark shadow crossed Rose's face. Her jaw visibly tightened. The idea that Terrence had come here at all, that he'd invaded Rose's space without her permission…it lit a fire in the pit of Cole's stomach.

"I've been trying to get him to leave for the last twenty minutes—"

"But we've been having so much fun."

"Terrence, the lady asked you to leave."

"It's a free country," Terrence said, picking up a flower carelessly from a nearby bucket with his greasy fingers. "Can't a guy come and look at some flowers and check out the pretty florist whenever the mood strikes him? Is that such a crime?"

Cole took two steps forward. His hands involuntarily clenched into fists. "It sounds like we've both asked you nicely. I would sincerely suggest that you hit the bricks, alright?"

"Why? You don't want all of the folks in Los Angeles to hear about your small-town side piece over here?"

That was the last straw. Before he could think better of it, before he could think at all, he plucked the camera out of Terrence's hands and smashed it against the hard flooring beneath his feet. Then, when Terrence didn't look sufficiently upset, Cole's fist rose to meet his jaw, wiping that arrogant smirk off of his face.

"Cole!" Rose gasped.

But he could barely hear her. For the moment, there was only the desire to keep her safe, to rip the man who'd spoken so cruelly about her out of her world. Rose had dealt with enough garbage in her life; she didn't need to deal with any more.

"And I don't want to see you around Rose Anderson again. Do you hear me?"

Terrence muttered something about lawyers and restraining orders, promises Cole didn't think he would keep. But when he finally stumbled out of the shop, Cole had to deal with the conflicted look on Rose's face, which was worse than any threat the tabloid photographer might have offered.

"Did you just *punch* that guy?"

"He deserved it. Did you hear what he said about you?"

"You can't just go around punching people and breaking their cameras!"

"I was defending you."

Cole's breath was short. His mind raced. She didn't...she wasn't happy with him? Or at least relieved that she wouldn't have to deal with Terrence ever again?

"Well, I don't need defending. I was doing perfectly fine on my own, thank you very much. You know, I'm not totally helpless."

"I know that."

"Really? You know that? Then why did you bully Annie and my sister into making up with me?"

Ah. That's what this was about. Cole looked at the floor. That night he'd run into Harper and Annie on the square, he'd just come from hearing Rose's story, the one about her lost, fake love and how it had broken her up inside. Cole hated the idea of her two closest friends abandoning her, not after she'd been carrying so many secrets alone for so long.

"I didn't bully them. I just wanted them to know that you were hurting, that it was wrong of them to leave you out in the cold with no one in your corner."

"I don't need anyone's help!" Rose snapped.

The control Cole had lost a moment ago? No, he hadn't found it yet. Cole really liked Rose, he felt things for Rose he hadn't been sure he was capable of feeling. Sure, those feelings were in their early stages—butterflies when she smiled at him, heat that spread across his cheeks whenever she called him on his junk, a strange obsession with her lips—but that didn't mean he was going to ignore a very real problem when she stared him in the face.

She had a gift. A great and beautiful and rare one that many people went through their lives without. There were people out there who cared about her. As much as he liked her, as much as he *did* sympathize with her desire for control over her own life and destiny, he couldn't quite wrap his mind around someone who gave love so freely but hid herself away whenever someone else tried to return the favor.

"I know you don't need it, but don't you want it?" He scoffed, the sound scraping the inside of his throat as he made it. "Hell, you have no idea what I wouldn't give for someone to help *me* out every once in a while. You have no idea what it's like to be alone in this world, do you? What it's like to have no one who cares about you until it's time to write them a check—"

Clang. The sound of the cowbell over the door shattered their tense conversation and dragged their attention straight for the doorway, where two figures stood framed with the sun at their backs, giving them the appearance of long, humanoid shadows. When they fully stepped inside, the light peering through the window caught their shined boots and polished badges and brimmed officers' hats. The one in front was older, more distinguished. A special patch had been ironed onto his left arm. Sheriff. The deputy behind him carried a pair of handcuffs, which jangled like spurs in an old western.

"Hiya, Rose," the one in the front said with a nod, though Cole got a feeling that behind his dark, tinted sunglasses, he'd never taken his eyes off of him.

"Hi, Sheriff. Is something the matter? Bouquet of daisies for your wife? I don't have any perfume in, but—"

"No, thank you, not this time." The man's hands went for his belt as he turned to face Cole, a true law enforcement power move. "I'm here for you, Mr. McKittrick."

"Is everything alright?"

"No, actually. You assaulted a man today, son. I've got to take you in."

All things considered, especially after all of the tabloid pieces he'd read in his lifetime about celebrities going to jail—Vivienne had even scrapbooked an article about Hugh Grant, of all people, getting arrested—Cole found the entire experience to be fairly painless. Sure, the small-town cops liked to shove their weight around. But when he'd been led through the center of town in handcuffs to a small building that looked more like a mid-range office space than a place to house lawbreakers and finally placed into a holding cell that might as well have been a tiny conference room, he couldn't help but marvel at how easy the whole process had been. They took his name, his prints, his statement, and then the beat cop and the sheriff who'd taken him in adjourned themselves for the coffee and fresh donuts waiting out in the bullpen for them.

This, he mused absentmindedly, was probably the most action any of the law enforcement in Hillsboro had seen in years. He didn't mind waiting in the holding cell for a few minutes if it meant they could have a donut to celebrate their successful capture of an actual criminal. As he sat in the stiff-backed plastic chair, his mind wandered. What did Rose think about him now? Was she still as angry with him as she had been when he'd swooped in? He hadn't meant to pull the whole damsel thing on her, but when he'd heard Terrence talking about Rose like she was nothing, like she was just some footnote in a crass story, he couldn't help the way his temper flared.

He didn't know how long he had been sat there, worrying about what she thought of him, when eventually, the door to his holding cell buzzed open, and the woman herself swept in. Her hair had long since fallen out of its braid, clinging to her neck and whipping about her ears as she closed the door behind him and rested against it.

"Cole? Oh my God, Cole! I can't believe they already have you in a holding cell," she breathed.

"Well, you know what they say. Justice is swift in a small town. Hey, you know, that might be a good line for the movie."

"I can't believe you're joking at a time like this."

He shrugged, still trying to feel her emotions out. "You know what they say, if life weren't funny, it would just be true."

Rose pressed her lips together in a fine line.

"I'm going to go talk to the sheriff. The bailiff let me in because I sell his wife flowers on the weekends, but I can't take you out with me. I'm sure the sheriff will sort all of this out."

"You don't have to—"

But before Cole could finish the protest, she'd already pressed the "call release" button on the door, which buzzed open remotely for her. With her hand on the latch, she turned over her shoulder and threw his own words back at him.

"Hey. You said you wanted someone in your corner, right? Let me be that someone."

"Okay. But you really don't have to or anything. It's good research. My character gets tossed in jail in the movie, too."

Cole waited. And waited. And waited. The twisting in his stomach, though, didn't go away. In spite of how angry she'd been with him, Rose had still gone to bat for him. She'd tried to be the person he'd thought he didn't have. A friend. His throat dried up and his breathing became more and more difficult in the small, darkened room.

But eventually, Rose made good on her promise, bringing the push-broom mustachioed sheriff back. The man opened the door, and began flipping idly through his file. Some crumbs hung loosely in his mustache, making him far less intimidating than he had been during his appearance at Rose's shop.

"Alright. Name?"

"Cole McKittrick."

"Mr. McKittrick. Is that your real name?"

Cole paused. Swallowed. "Uh, yeah."

It was a lie. But the sheriff didn't call him out on it.

"Are you aware that you ruined my favorite god-dang TV show?"

Rose's eyes widened. "Sheriff!"

"I know. I know. Not a crime." The man's flat lips didn't smile. In all seriousness, he continued to inspect the record in front of him before returning his entire attention to Cole. "Now, you understand why we brought you in here?"

"Yes, sir. I broke a man's camera and punched him in the face. But I was doing it in the defense of my girlfriend over there."

The sheriff's eyebrows shot towards his hairline. Rose echoed the action before she remembered to school her features into place.

"Girlfriend, huh? That's not what she told me." The sheriff leveled his gaze at the woman in question. "Now, Rose, you know only kinfolk and people in relationships are supposed to come into this here jail now and speak on behalf of the accused, don't you?"

That didn't sound like any law Cole knew of, but he wasn't going to argue with the man holding the key to his release. Small towns and their strange rules.

As the attention of the two men in her presence narrowed in on her, Rose cleared her throat and fought to put on a brave lying face. Cole knew her smile for what it was immediately: fake. But when she stepped into the room and took the seat beside him on the long bench lining the far wall, he tried his damnedest to match her pretense.

"No, we're definitely…I mean, we're absolutely…We're together."

The sheriff raised one eyebrow. "That so?"

"Yeah. I mean, look at us. We're practically a Hallmark card over here."

"You said you weren't dating."

Beside him, Cole could hear Rose's shallow, panicked breaths. More than anything, he wanted to reach out for her, but the cuffs around his wrist made such a thing basically impossible. Rose offered a tittering, slightly manic laugh before dipping into a decidedly more convincing speech. "Because what we have is so much deeper than that, Sheriff. It's more than just dating. It's real romance. See?"

And just like that, she kissed him. Their lips met in a perfect shock of emotion and sensation, and even though it was her only point of contact, Cole could feel her in every inch of himself, a beautiful sunrise creeping into even his coldest, darkest places. The instant they touched, he wanted more of her, wanted to feel her against him even tighter, wanted to know what it felt like to pin her and hold her and run his fingers through her hair as she breathed into him.

When she pulled away, he was breathless and confused and wanting, more than anything, for her to close the door on the sheriff and show him what her lips could *really* do. In a daze, he blinked, and tried to remain upright as his mind caught up with what his body had just experienced. Rose Anderson had kissed him. Rose Anderson had kissed him like he'd never been kissed before.

The sheriff coughed and shuffled his feet as Rose pulled away. Cole tried his best to give off the vibe that this—incredible, sensual, life-altering kissing—was something he did every day with the beautiful woman sitting beside him.

"Well. Now. Heh. McKittrick, seeing as you were defending the woman you love, and considering you've already offered to buy the man a new camera to replace the one you busted during your interview, I reckon it's okay if you go. I don't see any reason to continue with this whole thing."

"Really?" Cole asked, still slightly out of breath.

Either the sheriff was a romantic or he didn't want to be subject to anymore slightly PG-13 kissing sessions from the pair in his holding cell. Cole didn't care about the reason. All he cared about was the fact that the handcuffs were finally coming off.

"Yeah. And Rose, my wife's birthday's coming up. Do you figure you could mix me up one of your perfumes? She liked the Tuberose one from last year."

"I can do that. Mm-hm."

"Fantastic. Now, if I see either of you in here again, I'm not going to be such a sucker for young love, alright?"

They both muttered some variation of *yes, sir* before hustling out of the cell before he could change his mind. Together, Rose and Cole followed the man forward to the main office, a small collection of desks, American flags and aging laptops that served as the command center for the town's law enforcement. As they walked, though, the sheriff seemed deep in thought. Amused thought.

"Say, Rose," he said, when they reached the office and an over-sized pink box marked *JELLY'S DONUTS*. "You've already had a brush with the law, haven't you?"

A deep blush stained Rose's cheeks. She barely managed to look up from the floor. "I apologized and did my time. I would say that's the law working."

"Suppose you're right. Here. Take a donut for the road."

"Thanks, Sheriff."

Within a few moments and a few signed sheets of paper, they were out on the sidewalk in front of the town's lonely precinct. Cole rubbed his wrists as he struggled to keep up with Rose's brisk pace away from the station. She didn't seem very pleased to be here with him, but his mind couldn't really focus on that. Instead, he thought once again about Vivienne. It wasn't fair to compare the women in his life, he knew that. But he also knew that Vivienne would never have come to visit him in jail, much less rescue him from it. Not unless she thought maybe there were some cameras outside to witness their walk out of the doors. Rose had come without question. She'd helped him without asking for anything in return.

She'd even done the one thing she'd sworn never to do—kiss him and confirm their relationship in public—just to save his skin and get him out of there without issue.

He'd known she was kind. Selfless to a fault. But this was something else. A genuine act of kindness the likes of which he'd never experienced before.

Emotion welled up inside him, hot and fast. He tried to distract himself as best he could.

"What did he mean?"

"What?" Rose asked, a little bit breathless from marching back in the direction of her store so quickly.

"What did he mean back there, when he said you've had a brush with the law?"

A choked scoff from his walking companion. "You're welcome, by the way! If I hadn't come to rescue you, you'd still be stuck in that mess."

No arguing there. "Yeah, sure, but *what did he mean*? I have to know how Rose Anderson got thrown in the clink."

Only the *tap tap tap* of her shoes on the concrete responded for a few minutes. Even half a step behind her, he could see the blossoming blush grow across the back of her neck.

"There's a place in town called the Bronze Boot and they used to have one-dollar margarita nights."

"Why don't they have them anymore? What happened?"

"*I* happened. This group of tourists in from L.A. were talking smack about the Giants and I had to defend my team," Rose grumbled.

This was too good. Not only was the woman he'd been hanging out with a baseball fan, but a baseball fan who liked to get in slightly drunken brawls over the leader board? She was too good to be true. Too perfectly imperfect for words. He hung on her every word.

"What did you do?"

"Well, I swung at one of them and my aim wasn't so good."

"Right, because of all the tequila."

"Exactly. But he still pressed assault charges. I was the first one in the family to go in the police log. My mother cried for a week straight. I had to make a formal apology and pick up trash for a weekend. Thankfully, the people of Hillsboro are very environmentally conscious and so there was barely anything for me to do."

"You know what? You surprise me more and more every day, Rose Anderson. I think I could be with you a thousand years and still, you'd amaze me."

It was true. But the line was a test. A piece of bait dangled out in front of her. He wanted her to hear in those words everything he couldn't say out loud. *Please. You kissed me. Tell me that means something. Tell me that you want me and that I should throw away everything to be with you. Help me make the decision I know is coming.* But she didn't do anything of the kind. Instead, she fished her keys out of her purse and remained steadfastly silent as they closed the distance to her shop, which loomed large overhead when they landed on the sidewalk in front of it. He'd hoped that her tipsy fighting story might have opened *her* up, but no. She was as unreachable as she had been since the moment they left the station.

"So," he asked, to break the silence as she opened the lock, "does getting tossed up in a police cell and making you break me out qualify as 'shared experience?'"

"You know what, Cole? After today, I think we can consider your chemistry lessons finished."

With that, Rose Anderson entered her shop, slammed the door behind her, tossed the "Open" sign to "Closed," and left Cole on the sidewalk. He tried not to think too often in metaphors, but it was hard to ignore a sign as explicit as that.

Chapter Fifteen

Rose

Rose survived her dust-up with the cameraman without any major physical damage, but she couldn't deny the damage that the last few days had done to her heart. She'd gone from hating Cole for trying to manage her life like everyone else did, to getting rescued by him, to *kissing him* in front of the entire Hillsboro Police Station. Not that the police station was very big—three officers and a dog made up the entire police force during any given shift—but still.

The next day, when she rolled into work wearing her prescription sunglasses and carrying an oversized, overpriced iced coffee in one hand, she couldn't stop thinking about it. Couldn't stop thinking about him and that kiss and the way it had made her weak in the knees.

And weak in the heart.

For goodness' sake, her lips were tingling as if she'd only just come up for air, rather than the truth, which was that not only had she stopped kissing him half a day ago, but she'd also spent an inordinate amount of time in the shower last night running her washcloth over her lips. As if she could scrub the feeling of him away.

When she finally ambled up to the shop, she blinked behind her sunglasses. She'd expected at least a day of silence from Cole. She thought he might have the decency to keep to himself for at least twenty-four hours so they could both shove down the embarrassment they were both probably feeling after yesterday's little display and her total breaking of the rules.

But, no. As ever, he was painfully against following any sort of convention she'd set out for him; his shoulders and his personality always proved too big to fit into any kind of box where she might have shoved him. Standing there by the doorway with his back to her, she checked the reflection in the doorway glass to see what he was doing. He held two slightly unwieldy things in his arms—a bright, pink box with a familiar logo and a brown paper bag from the bookshop down the street—and struggled to hold a black marker pen cap in his mouth so he could haphazardly scribble something on the top of the pink box.

It would have been funny if she wasn't still kind of mad with him for barging into her life and forcing Harper and Annie to apologize to her. It also would have been cute…if she weren't trying very, very hard not to think of him that way.

Or maybe…a decision fluttered on delicate, butterfly's wings in her chest. Yesterday, he'd kissed her like he didn't want to stop. He was always dropping little flirtatious comments about the way she looked or how big her heart was or why she hadn't been "scooped up" by some lucky guy yet.

As she stood there, staring blankly at the man wrestling a note onto an oversized donut box, she couldn't help but wonder: what if Cole felt the same way about her? What if they were *both* growing to care for each other, but neither of them wanted to admit it because they both thought the other one didn't want to? What if they were losing their chance to be together because they were too afraid to take a little chance?

Warmth blossomed in Rose's chest.

"What are you doing here?"

At the sound of her voice, Cole jumped, spun on his heel, and stared at her as though she'd caught him red-handed in the middle of a heist. "What are *you* doing here? You weren't supposed to be here for another twenty minutes."

"I couldn't sleep. Now, answer the question."

"It was supposed to be a surprise."

He gestured to the pieces in his arm. Rose stared at them, skeptically.

"For me?"

"Breakfast and a book. I saw all of your perfume stuff at your house and your sister told me that you might want to do it professionally someday. I kept wanting to ask about it, but I didn't want to seem like I was interfering—"

He trailed off with a little shrug, leaving them both to stew in the silence of the street. Rose, though, couldn't take her eyes off of the box. He'd gotten her breakfast and a book. Sure, she'd broken him out of jail yesterday, but still...this practically knocked her backwards.

"I can't believe you did this."

"Too much? I'm sorry. It's—"

"Cole McKittrick, any woman who doesn't have chemistry with you must be a statue or something. Why are you here with me taking lessons if you already think to do things like this?"

He opened and closed his mouth. Rose watched the indecision in his eyes and before he even said anything, she knew. Vivienne. All of this—everything between them—went right back to Vivienne.

"This is what boyfriends are supposed to do. Even fake ones. Especially fake ones who screwed up as badly as I did yesterday."

Supposed to, sure. But when was the last time a guy did something like this for her? Even back when she'd thought she was in a swoon-worthy, stars-falling romance, no one had done a grand gesture like this. The bookstore didn't even open for another hour; he must have called in favors to make this happen.

Rose ducked her head as she made a beeline for the shop door, which she easily opened with her handy ring of keys.

"So, the book and the breakfast weren't romantic gestures; they were apologies."

"No, they were romantic gestures. Vivienne wasn't really one for romantic gestures. She didn't like all of that stuff. I thought maybe I was a little rusty. Needed some practice with my wooing."

Well, there was no use in getting sentimental about it. Going through the motions of her morning routine, she tried to remain as detached and professional as possible.

"But I *do* owe you an apology. For meddling with your sister and Annie. And for getting myself thrown in jail."

That last part required no apology. Sure, Rose wanted to go back in time and erase the kiss from her memory, *Men in Black* style, but with the paparazzo harassing her, she hadn't minded Cole swooping in a little and saving the day. Sure, she *could* handle herself, but it was nice—flattering, even—that he would risk his relationship with the press to protect her.

But there was still that one thing…that one thing that the reporter had said that struck a chord with her. That hung in her mind even now. It dominated her thoughts almost as much as the kiss had.

"Lady, you don't know everything about him. You'd better be careful." That's what he'd said before Cole had arrived. Those were the words she couldn't shake.

"Well, seeing as you're still my only option for my sister's engagement party, I'll forgive you under two conditions," Rose said, only half-teasing.

"Anything," Cole replied.

Her heart fluttered a little at the way he said that. She fought to contain the sensation.

"First, never use the word *wooing* again."

"But it's in the novels," Cole protested.

"And second…" She trailed off as she slipped into her uniform apron and scuttled behind the safety of the counter. "That guy yesterday. Before he showed up, he said that I didn't know everything about you. What am I missing?"

Something flashed across Cole's face, but it was gone by the time she blinked. "He's a gossip columnist and photo hound. He's just trying to get a rise out of us. Both of us."

The explanation made sense, but something about it didn't sit right with Rose. Maybe she was just paranoid. Maybe she was overthinking it. But…it didn't sound like the truth to her. At least, not the entire truth.

"Come on, Cole. You know all of the embarrassing details of my life. Tell me a little bit about yours."

"Everything there is to know about me has been written over and over again in the press. You can google it faster than I can tell you."

He said it all with that same charming smile of his. But as he went for the broom and began sweeping without her even asking him to do it, Rose followed him with her eyes and noticed that he never looked up to meet them. He was hiding from her. When she realized he wasn't going to stop hiding, she turned back to the sketches she'd done yesterday for the floral arrangements for May's engagement party.

"Google doesn't have the whole story, I'm sure. Like, why did you get into acting?"

"You're not going to believe it. No one ever does."

"Try me."

"I never wanted to do something in movies and television. I was born and raised in Los Angeles, but I always thought I'd do, you know, carpentry or something. Something with my hands."

So far, there wasn't anything entirely incredible or unbelievable about that story. Something in his face seemed off. Not quite right, but since she couldn't put her finger on what, exactly, the problem was, Rose waited patiently for the twist.

"But I had tons of friends who were actors, and one day, my friend asks me to give him a ride to an audition. Sure, no problem. And when we get there to the lot, the casting director's kid is outside on her day off from school. So, my friend goes inside. I stay outside. And the little girl asks if I know how to do a cartwheel."

"And did you?"

"I am a *champion* cartwheeler, Rose," he said, with that mock arrogance of his. "So, I'm out there, showing her how it's done, and the casting agent comes outside. Likes the look of me, and asks if I've ever done any acting before. The rest, as they say, is history."

Strange as the story was, Rose believed it. Over the years, she'd heard stranger stories about Hollywood from Annie, and almost all of those turned out to be true.

"Sounds like a fairy tale. Your parents must have been so proud."

"Yeah. Definitely. You wouldn't believe it. They're the celebrities of their neighborhood. Text me every time I'm on TV."

That reply came out too fast. He kept his attention on the floor. Time to change the subject, no matter how painful the new topic would be.

"And Vivienne? Did she like the show?"

A pause. Even the broom in his hands stopped sweeping. When he did eventually speak, Rose could barely hear him.

"I…You know, we never really talked about that. About whether or not she liked the show."

"Have you heard from her?"

Rose tried not to think about the fact that at the question, Cole lit up like a Fourth of July firework, brightening at the mere mention of her.

"Yeah, after we got caught on our movie date. I think this is really working, you know. She's really coming around, seeing me as a real choice again. And with your help and the romance novels and this movie…It's all going to be perfect. Thanks, Rose."

A million thoughts flashed in Rose's mind. The kiss. The way he held her hand and the way they'd baked pies together and the way he made her feel like, for the first time, she could actually be herself, flaws and anger and feelings and all.

Despite all the precautions they'd taken, she realized that she had feelings for him. And they were never going to be returned.

She needed some way to correct them.

"Well. Actually, after the paparazzi guy came over yesterday, I had an idea. Do you trust me?"

"Of course I do."

But something—an instinct, maybe—told Rose that wasn't entirely true.

After that conversation, as the day went on Rose closed her heart off to the possibility of more. Sure, there had been a brief, shining moment in there where she'd thought…*Maybe*. Maybe if he kissed her back like he had the day before, then maybe it was possible for him to like her, to care about her, to maybe be able to fall in love with her.

It was a stupid dream. A fool's fantasy. And it proved once again that she was not the kind of person who could be trusted with the keys to her own heart. The last guy she'd been in love with hadn't existed; the one she'd caught herself falling for was in love with someone else.

Go figure.

But, she reminded herself for the thousandth time as they made the drive to the Miller's Pond, being his friend would be enough. There were countless people in this world who would never have a friend as kind and thoughtful and charismatic as Cole McKittrick was. She should be happy with his friendship. It should have been enough.

And it was that friendship—that, and absolutely nothing else, she assured herself—that brought them to the pond that night.

Normally, by this time of night, Rose would have been comfortably tucked in bed, either with a cup of tea and a good book, or fast asleep with the family's cat (Bermondsey) and the dog (Stella) soundly cuddled into various parts of her comforter. Tonight, though, she couldn't even think about something as remote and impossible as sleep. Who could sleep when they were about to go skinny-dipping?

Well, they weren't *actually* going to go skinny-dipping. Instead, they were going to try to convince other people that they were.

When Rose finally pulled the car up in a small clearing near the pond, Cole read a nearby sign with delighted laughter dancing on his lips.

"The Miller's Pond. *That's* why you wanted me to wear a bathing suit? I was afraid you were going to trick me into more fishing."

"I thought we might go for a swim," Rose said with a shrug as she reached into the back of the truck cab for supplies. Towels. Flashlights. A can of hard seltzer for a little bit of liquid courage. That sort of thing.

When they were out of the car a moment later, Cole couldn't hold back his teasing. Even in the face of all of the moon-soaked beauty around them, he kept his focus set squarely on her as they walked down the dock that hung out over the water.

"Rose Anderson, you surprise me."

"Not skinny-dipping," she hissed, hating that she was even saying the words out loud. "Just a normal, everyday swim."

"I think you mean every *night* swim."

Against her better judgment, Rose's lips twisted into a smirk. Okay, she could admit it. Cole had a good ear for puns. Game recognized game, as they said. As they walked, she slipped out of her simple dress, and into her bathing suit as Cole slipped out of his shirt, leaving him only in his loose-fitting swim shorts.

The moonlight suited him. She couldn't deny that. If she'd been another kind of woman—bolder, braver, more willing to fight for what she wanted—she would have kissed him right then and there, pressing herself into him and feeling every inch of him against every inch of her, exploring his body until they both knew that they were right for each other.

The urge was so strong that, by the time they reached the end of the dock, which led off directly into the deepest part of the pond, Rose couldn't help herself. Not from jumping his bones, but by disposing of them.

"You really are impossible. Get in the water."

And with that, she pushed him into the pond. But in the three point five seconds it took his surprised body to flail into the inky depths, Rose heard three words that ruined everything, sending her straight into eleventh grade lifeguard mode.

"Rose! Rose! I can't swim!"

"What?"

His head popped above the dark waters for only a moment before slipping down under again.

Without a moment's hesitation, Rose dove in after him. Her body broke the plane of the warm water, which clung to her like a second skin as she knifed through it, searching for the flailing man she'd just accidentally tried to drown.

The pond sat near a series of shifting tectonic plates, keeping it a balmy temperature all year round, which was good for year-round skinny-dippers, but even better for Rose right now. It meant that Cole's body wouldn't have gone into shock yet, he wouldn't have—

Gotcha. She grabbed his hard, solid body and fought them both up towards air. Saving his life was no time to think about how right his form felt against hers, of course, but the thought did cross her mind and the press of his against her body awakened every one of her nerve endings.

As soon as they both reached the breathable surface, Rose forced her eyes open, ignoring the sting in them.

"Are you—"

But that's when she realized. He wasn't flailing anymore. He wasn't fighting the water or its pull. He was treading water perfectly fine. And smirking at her as though he'd just pulled a fantastic joke.

"Gotcha."

"You absolute snake! You almost gave me a heart attack!"

"And you almost gave me a heart attack. Have you seen how you look in that bathing suit? I know it's not any of my business, but the fact that you haven't found your Person yet is just…It's beyond me."

"I could say the same thing about you."

Rose's throat tightened up. She was wrong about that, wasn't she? He *had* found his Person? The Vivienne woman was beautiful and smart, a true humanitarian from her online profiles. Sure, she didn't seem like the warm and romantic type that Cole deserved, but he really seemed to care about her. He *had* found his Person. And it was her job—*as his friend*—to make sure that the two ended up together. No matter what she thought about it.

Swimming closer to him, she started to say something about that, when, from across the lake, a flash like lightning shattered the still, dark, tranquility of the water. *Flash! Flash! Flash!* Not heat lightning. Not real lighting, but camera flashes.

Cole immediately sprung into action. "Hey! Hey! What are you doing?"

And just like that, leaving as quickly as he'd arrived, the dark figure across the pond was gone. Cole began swimming across, as if he was going to manage catching the man on the motorcycle on bare foot. Rose swallowed back a laugh.

"Cole."

"What?" he asked, spinning around to face her. Even in the moonlight, which usually robbed the rich landscape of Hillsboro of its color at this time of night, Rose could clearly see that his face was soaked red with rage. Her eyes softened.

"Don't go after him."

"And why the hell wouldn't I? He invaded our—"

She swallowed and shrugged, or shrugged as much as she was capable of while treading water like this. Her voice was a little weaker than she'd expected or wanted it to be. "I called him."

"You *what*?"

"I called him. You wanted to get Vivienne's attention, right?"

"Right."

"You told me that this afternoon, so I pulled a little bit of an Annie move. Skin-colored bathing suit. Full moon. Cameraman. They'll *think* we were skinny-dipping. And the headlines will most certainly make their way to Los Angeles."

It had seemed a simple enough plan when she'd thought it out this morning. If he wanted to make his ex-girlfriend jealous enough to come to Hillsboro and take him back, then it stood to reason that if she saw him getting supremely cozy with some girl, then that might be enough to drive her out here. Cole swam close to her, close enough that there was nothing between them but the steam rising up from the placid surface of the lake.

"You did this…For me?"

"I know it's not exactly the most ethical thing. I probably should have asked you first, but…"

He smiled at her then, in the full light of the moon, with the crystalline reflection of the water dancing in his eyes, and she knew she'd made a mistake.

She'd done exactly the right thing, and in doing it, she'd lost her chance with him.

"No. It's great. It's perfect. Thank you."

What a coincidence that he would say so. Because that's what Rose kept reminding herself every other minute. Every time her heart wanted to jump out of her chest and run straight in his direction.

That was the problem with tonight. She'd thought it was going to get him out of her system. That she would have one night of closeness, one night of sweetness, one unforgettable night under the stars with him and then be able to forget him forever.

But the exact opposite was true. Instead of getting out of her system, he'd become part of it. And she didn't think she'd be able to shake him any time soon.

Later that night, Rose somehow managed to drive blindly back to the house. Thank God for muscle memory, because otherwise, she certainly would have crashed from the wall of tears currently building up in her eyes. For the first time, she desperately wished for her own apartment. Her own space. The loft was no longer enough for her. She craved an apartment where only the walls and her pictures would be there to hear her cry.

The situation only got worse when she parked the car, staggered up the front steps, and found her mother sitting on the porch swing, clutching her phone to her chest. Rose tried to sneak through the shadows, but the traitorous squeaking of the porch floorboards gave her away. Her mother roused from her dozing and leapt to her feet.

"Rose! We had half the town out looking for you! Your father and Harper and Annie are out there still—"

Somewhere between the second and third step, Rose's legs had stopped working. They'd just run out of gas or hope or the will to keep moving. Her mother paused, momentarily and uncharacteristically at a loss for words. Then, her tone softened from angered worry to deeply confused concern. "Rose…? What's wrong?"

Rose opened her mouth. But only a choked sob made its way out at first. Her knees gave out under her, and slowly, she sunk and sunk and sunk until she was nothing more than a crumple of a girl on the front porch steps. "Mom…I think maybe I'm falling in love."

"That's wonderful! Oh, my dear, I am so happy for you! You've finally done it. This is just…This is so wonderful."

But when Rose's mother came to sit beside her and take her in her arms, the floodgates opened. The tears fell. She'd stupidly let herself fall in love, realize it too late, and lose it before she'd even had the chance to pursue it. For once, her mother didn't fuss when Rose left tear stains on her blouse.

"No, Mom. No, it's not."

Chapter Sixteen

Cole

The pictures hit the internet that night. And when Cole woke up the next morning, he knew that Vivienne Matilde had made her way into town. If he'd been the sentimental type, he might have said his heart told him that she'd flown to his side, ready to make up after so much time apart. If he'd been the poetic type, he might have said he felt a shift in the air that could only be linked to someone he loved so deeply.

But he was a realist. Not even the stack of romance novels or the steady prescription dose of romcoms Rose shoveled in his direction were enough to change that. And as a realist, he knew that Vivienne was in town because his agent, his manager, his personal trainer and a host of press agents had blown up his phone so thoroughly that its vibrating, and not his alarm, was what woke him that morning.

Oh, and also because the hotel manager called him from the first floor and informed him that a woman with nine Louis Vuitton suitcases was currently sitting in the lobby, waiting for him to escort her to her room. The manager wanted to know if he should contact the local authorities.

The offer was slightly tempting. Not because he wanted Vivienne thrown into jail or anything, but because he would have liked to see intense, hard-headed Vivienne Matilde going up against the equally intense local sheriff. A bout like that could have made him millions in ticket sales.

Instead, he told the front desk clerk that he would be down in a minute, got dressed, and started for the lobby. Strangely, his feet didn't move as lightly or as quickly as he'd imagined when he'd dreamed about this particular reunion.

Mostly because he was thinking about Rose.

The kiss that they'd shared hadn't been the most romantic. After all, it had been against the backdrop of a jail cell. But it had changed something in him, awakened a possibility he'd thought dormant. No one kissed like that if they weren't interested. That kiss Rose gave him had meant *something*, and when he'd brought her breakfast and a book the morning after to apologize, he'd hoped that maybe she would see something in him—something that maybe she could love. He'd thought it was one of those romance novel gestures where the heroine would suddenly realize *oh, he's the one*.

He'd taken a chance. It was a chance she didn't answer. So, when she'd skinny-dipped through the tabloids with him—when she'd been the one to *arrange* it—he had to assume that the door on him and Rose Anderson had been closed.

As the elevator descended towards the lobby and towards the woman he'd been trying to win back for six months now, he tried to remind himself of that. Tried to remind himself that Rose clearly wasn't interested, and as such, he needed to focus on someone who was.

Sure, through his time with Rose, Cole had realized that Vivienne had never exactly been the warm, loving woman he'd wanted. But she was here. She was interested. And she fit his life. That mattered, too.

When the gilt elevator doors opened wide, revealing the rustic-chic lobby beyond—complete with decorative cowhide throws, poured concrete walls and Edison bulbs as far as the eye could see—focusing on Vivienne proved remarkably easy. Not only was she standing in the absolute center of the expansive yet cozy lobby, surrounded by a stack of luggage almost as tall as she was, but she was also giving the manager quite the earful.

Cole internally cringed but didn't dare to let his reaction show on his face. Vivienne was one of those people for whom *I'd like to speak to your manager* had been invented, and she dropped that phrase almost as often as she dropped the names of her more famous friends. He'd always thought that she just needed to relax, that she just needed someone who could be there to soften her hard edges a bit. Now, he knew that there wasn't anything he could do but interject as seamlessly as he could.

"Vivienne! What are you doing here?" he asked, shooting a warning, *I'm a distraction and I'd run if I were you* glance to the manager over her shoulder. As soon as Vivienne's back was turned, the man retreated, posthaste, to his small, locked office behind the floating front desk.

Once Vivienne turned around, she slipped the sunglasses off of her eyes and immediately fell into her default Los Angeles fawn.

"Cole?" She blinked, ostensibly to let her eyes adjust to the light, though he knew better. She was buying time to size him up, to see if the man who she'd left months ago was doing better or worse in the times since they'd been together. He might have been insulted if he hadn't done the same. To his slight disappointment, she didn't have a strand of hair or eyelash out of place, meaning she was exactly the same as when he'd last seen her.

"Oh, Cole it *is* you. My knight in shining armor. Thank you so much for coming down. That manager wouldn't let me see you. Isn't that ridiculous? Well, I told him that if he wanted me out of this lobby, then he needed to call you right away because I knew you would sort this whole thing out. My room is 1221. Where are you?"

"The penthouse."

He hadn't meant for that to come across as bragging as it sounded but being in Vivienne's presence again was arresting. So many warring emotions invaded him, fighting for his attention. Anger at the way she'd left him. Disappointment at the way she'd returned. Anxiety about the beautiful woman who'd made this whole thing possible.

And, yes. Considering the way their relationship had ended, he did feel a little entitled to the penthouse brag. The way her mouth dropped open in slight surprise made the guilt he felt at flexing on her all worthwhile.

"Ah, that's why they wouldn't give it to me. I insisted on the penthouse, but they don't even have a *suite* available, can you believe that? I've had to take a normal room like some kind of pleb. Apparently," she said, shooting a venomous look at the manager, "they don't even have an illuminated mirror in there. Thank God I thought to bring my own."

"There are a lot of people in town for the shoot. It's pretty busy here. I'm sure it wasn't anything personal."

That's how she took it, though. Her perfect, print magazine perfect face scrunched up into a dismissive glare of displeasure. Lowering her voice as though she didn't want to offend the certainly already offended staff, she leaned in closer to him.

"I mean, I realize that, but you'd think they'd want to treat certain clientele with a bit more care. Anyway. Small towns. I shouldn't expect the same level of service here that I would in L.A. Just a failure to manage my expectations, I guess."

At that, she brushed away invisible dust from her pressed, wide-leg tan trousers. They were part of what Cole called her *fussy casual* collection, the uniforms she put on when she wanted everyone to *think* she was relaxed and cool, when in reality, she'd spent forty-five minutes measuring and folding the cuff on the right pants leg. When Cole didn't say anything and couldn't think of anything intelligent to say, she tittered a small, almost self-deprecating laugh.

No, not self-deprecating. She was deprecating him and his lack of response.

"Aren't you going to say hello? I came all of this way."

"Hello, Vivienne. It's…" He trailed off, the sentence tapering as he searched for the words to adequately describe everything going through his mind right now. This was what he'd wanted. For her to show up and pretend it was her idea. For her to want him back so badly that she'd brave the wilderness that was Hillsboro. And parts of him still did want that. Parts of him wanted to go up to the roof and crow about how he'd won, about how he'd showed her that he wasn't as worthless as she'd seemed to think him six months ago. But there were more parts of him—stronger, bolder, more intense—that just…didn't feel anything when he looked at her. Finally, he settled on just giving the polite, expected reply. "It's good to see you."

"You don't seem so sure."

"No, of course I'm glad to see you. I'm just…" *I'm just wondering if a couple of paparazzi pictures of me "skinny-dipping" were really all it took to get you out here.* "I guess I'm just wondering what brought all of this on. I can't believe you're here. I'm just in shock, I guess."

"A happy surprise, I hope."

Words failed him yet again. This time, he just nodded.

"Well," Vivienne continued without invitation. Carefully, she adjusted the handbag currently nestled into the crook of her elbow. "I told you I needed to get out of L.A. After a while, the heat can be just oppressive."

"Any other reason?"

That hung in the air. She glanced up at him from under her unnaturally long eyelashes, the ones he knew she'd spent hours in a doctor's office getting artificially enhanced because—as she once told him—men are suckers for the doe-eyed look. The eyelashes, she argued, had been a business expense, like a cell phone or a top of the line computer. A tool she used to get what she wanted.

She fluttered those lashes at him now; her red lips puckered into a pout.

"I'm really transparent, aren't I?"

"Just a little bit."

"Well, Cole, I came here to talk to you about something very serious. Something I just couldn't say over the phone."

"And that is?"

She winced, then looked around the small lobby. He noticed that her eyes flickered to the elevator, but instead of suggesting that they go upstairs, she motioned to the small waiting set-up behind them.

"Can we sit down?" she asked.

Cole didn't exactly want to agree, but gracefully extracting himself from this situation was impossible. He knew that it was a trick before they'd even made their first move to sit. But when he seated himself on one of the plush, oversized couches, he didn't have any choice but to stay there when she nestled up beside him, too close to be polite. He could feel the heat radiating off of her body; the air between them reeked of her face powder and thick perfume.

The closeness felt like a betrayal of Rose, like he would be humiliated if she walked in and saw them this close. *She doesn't want you*, he reminded himself, trying to put on a brave face for the woman who very much did seem to want him. *She wants you to be with Vivienne.*

"Cole, I know the way things ended didn't go quite right for us, but I have always cared for you. You know that, don't you?"

It hadn't felt like she cared for him, but he nodded anyway with a smile that he hoped came across as confident and easy. "Yeah. Sure, I know that."

"And because I care about you so much, and since I have so many ties to the press, I've been keeping a really close eye on you during this whole film shoot thing. When I found out you were coming here early, I knew that it was a recipe for trouble. I got so worried about you. About your career. I mean, the movie's big step in the right direction and everything, but—"

"What do you mean?"

"I mean that you've…" Vivienne once again adjusted her grip on her handbag, adjusting the antique tortoiseshell handles and letting them clack against her freshly painted and buffed nails. "Well, you're in a very precarious place in your career right now, aren't you? You could skyrocket to the top, be the celebrity you deserve to be, or you could plummet down into obscurity. And, Cole, I desperately don't want the latter to happen to you. And, if I can say it…to us."

Cole couldn't help the small laugh that escaped him. *I don't want you to go plummeting into obscurity* wasn't quite *I still love you.* "Thanks," he replied, dryly.

That's when Vivienne stopped messing with the handbag and instead, reached out one of those perfect, soft, tender, ice-cold hands to him. She wrapped her fingers around his wrist, holding him like she didn't ever want to let go. Like she regretted having let go in the first place. Her look turned severe.

"Which is why I've come to warn you."

"Warn me?"

"That girl that you've been photographed with. I'm sure she is just *so* nice. Incredibly lovely. She looks beautiful and sweet from every picture that I've seen." There was a pause. Cole waited for the inevitable turn, all while he stared down at the place where her hand touched his, the place where he didn't feel sparks or lightning or anything he felt when Rose touched him. When Vivienne touched him, he felt nothing but the weight of her hand against his skin. "But, Cole, you left *Crime Spree: Beach City* and all of that money and all of that fame because you said you wanted to be a bigger star.

You traded everything for a chance at being greater than you were before. I don't want to see you waste that on some fling."

"Rose isn't just some fling," Cole said, harsher than he'd intended.

Obviously, that wasn't exactly true. He and Rose had always intended for their relationship to be disposable, one that they could toss aside as soon as they'd both gotten everything they wanted. Still, to think of her as something as tawdry as a "fling" didn't sit right with him.

"Everyone thinks that when they've just started to feel things for someone. But I want you to think in the long-term. Shouldn't you be with someone who cares about your career? About your future? Isn't that what you want?"

It was what he was supposed to want. He knew that much. He was supposed to want picture-perfect, camera-ready Vivienne and all of her industry connections. He wasn't supposed to want Rose, who apparently was so ready to get rid of him that she staged paparazzi photos implying they'd both skinny-dipped.

When he didn't answer, couldn't answer, Vivienne smiled a gentle smile that reminded him of everything he'd once loved about her. Beneath her exterior, she *was* kind. She really did care about people. She just didn't care about them in the way that Rose and the Andersons did. She wanted people to succeed at any cost, feelings and consequences be damned.

It would have been admirable if it wasn't currently tearing him apart.

"I know it's a bit presumptuous of me, considering how things ended with us, but I've broken things off with Tyson."

That made Cole's ears perk up. Tyson had been one of Cole's co-stars on the *Crime Spree: Beach City*…His relationship with

Vivienne also happened to have significant overlap with Cole's. When Vivienne had officially left, she'd made it clear why she'd chosen Tyson over him. Those reasons didn't seem particularly flexible. Cole swallowed.

"When did that happen?"

"It doesn't matter. He didn't understand me like you did. And I could never understand him the way that I understand you."

Did she understand him at all? Cole used to think so. He used to think she was the perfect person for him, the calm, reasonable center in the slightly repressed sea of his emotions. Now...he wasn't so sure.

And it was the uncertainty that killed him.

"You don't have to give me an answer now. I'll be staying in Hillsboro as long as it takes. But you and I...We've always made sense, Cole. We fit. And if you want someone who will be there for you long after you leave Hillsboro, then..." She gave a slight squeeze to his wrist before taking her hand back. "I'll be waiting."

"Thank you, Vivienne." It was all he could say.

As Vivienne rose to her feet, she never let her eyes slip from him, not even for a second. "You really *do* feel something for your small-town girl, don't you?"

It was Cole's turn to falter in his words, to take too many meaningful pauses. "It's...complicated."

"That was the thing about you and me, Cole. They could say a lot of things about us, but complicated wasn't one of them."

"Yeah, I guess you're right," he lied, mostly just to get her out of his immediate vicinity, so he could once again think with a clear head. Funny how two people could have two such different takes on how a relationship had gone.

"Well." Vivienne straightened to her full height and tossed her head. In a flash, all traces of the slightly vulnerable woman she'd been a moment before vanished. She was, once again, all soft, toothy smiles and all business. "Will you walk me up to my room?"

Cole checked his watch. Plenty of time, but he'd use his excuse since he had one. "I'd love to, but I promised Rose I would meet her for breakfast. It's her sister's engagement party in a few days and I think she wanted to show me some of her dress choices or something."

A lie. Breakfast was true, but the dress thing was a lie. He just wanted to make himself seem even *less* available than he really was.

Vivienne's laugh was apparently supposed to convince him she was joking, but all it did was make him wonder if she really was as jealous as she seemed. "Already choosing her over me, huh?"

"I made a promise. I'm just trying to keep it."

Vivienne tutted as she waved one of the bellhops over to her mountain of luggage. Her perfect construction of hair didn't move an inch when she shook her head at him.

"Oh, my dear, sweet Cole. You always were a sucker."

Chapter Seventeen

Rose

That morning, the town of Hillsboro wasn't just abuzz with rumors and gossip and conversations and slightly exaggerated or completely made up stories.

It was practically aflame.

Everywhere Rose went—from her own breakfast table to the quaint coffee shop where Cole had asked to meet her for a breakfast debrief before she started her shift at the shop—the eyes of the populace followed her, cataloguing everything from her posture to how tired she seemed to be, gauging whether the pictures they'd seen online were telling the truth.

Had Rose Anderson gone wild? Had she finally joined the rest of the town and finally had a lakeside, moonlight-soaked fling?

In any other circumstance, Rose might have relished the sudden change in her fortunes. If she'd known that this was all it would take for people to stop whispering about her like some sort of romance-deprived sad sack, she would have gone pretend skinny-dipping years ago. As it was, from the moment she woke up with baggy, red-rimmed and puffy eyes, her heart ached with every beat. Her mother's counsel the night before hadn't helped, nor had a good, long cry. And today, she didn't just have to face the rest of the town.

She had to face Cole, too.

Cole, the man she now knew she was starting to fall for. The man she'd foolishly thought she could push away. Every time she thought of their escapade the night before, her stomach felt as if she was suddenly back on that water again, leaving her feeling slightly buoyant in addition to slightly seasick.

But when she saw him again, their usual coffee orders sitting on the counter in the middle of the crowded shop, all of that melted away. Her anxieties and worries took a back seat to that jolt of electricity that took hold of her every time he smiled in her direction.

She knew it was ridiculous to think that anything could happen between them, especially after what she'd done last night, but there was that persistent, nettling hope inside of her that wouldn't die. The hope that everything would work out okay, that hope that maybe after last night, he would realize that he hadn't wanted anyone else. That she was the only woman in the world for him.

Eventually, she settled into her seat at the little corner table where Cole was currently sipping coffee and flipping through his screenplay. First day of filming was soon, and they chattered idly about everything *but* the skinny-dipping elephant in the room. But then, when he closed the script and looked at her—really looked at her—she got the definite sense that something was wrong.

"So…Vivienne got into town this morning. She saw the pictures online last night and caught a seat on the plane one of the film's producers was using to fly in this morning."

Rose's heart sunk. All of the light that had entered her upon seeing Cole again promptly dimmed; the electricity cooled. *This* was why everyone had been staring. People had been watching her carefully, but not saying anything, because they knew something she didn't. They knew about the paparazzi pictures from last night, *and* they knew that Vivienne was now in town.

Rose swallowed and took a long, deep sip of her hazelnut and caramel macchiato. It was too hot and scalded her tongue, then burned as it trickled down the back of her throat. She didn't care.

"Oh, really? So, our plan worked, then, I guess?"

"I saw her this morning. She seems..." Cole shot her a flat, slightly amused look over the pages of his script. "Very eager."

"Good. That's great, Cole."

Try as she might, she couldn't get the words to come out genuinely. On the one hand, she knew that this was what Cole wanted. He'd told her about his plan to get Vivienne back; that meant he couldn't possibly want her instead. On the other hand, her heart cared about him. Deeply. *She* cared about him. Selfishly, she didn't want to lose him.

Cole's lips quirked up in that easy, piercing way of his. "You don't seem so sure."

Rose assessed the situation, scanning the rest of the coffee shop, which was full of customers currently trying *very* hard to make it look like they weren't eavesdropping.

"Let's take these to go. I have a question for you, but I don't really know if you want to answer it in front of all of these people."

"It's okay," Cole said, too confident. "No one's paying attention to us."

"Cole, *everyone* is paying attention to us."

Rose didn't say anything for a while, giving him the opportunity to hear the way the entire shop was mostly quiet, trying to catch every word that they were saying to one another.

"Okay, let's move."

A few minutes later, away from the oppressively friendly atmosphere of the coffee shop, Rose and Cole walked along the train tracks that cut across the back half of town. The trains in these parts were so rare that people had lately taken to calling it *Influencers' Mile*, on account of all of the wannabe social media stars who came out here for impromptu photo shoots. With the trees all around the track practically glowing bronze with the sun filtering through their changing fall leaves, Rose didn't blame them. It was beautiful here.

"So," Cole asked, when he was sure that they were totally alone. "What did you want to ask me?"

The crunch of leaves and the rustle of stones beneath their feet underscored Rose's sizing up of her fake boyfriend. Vivienne was in town, yet she didn't see any change in him. What was he thinking? What was he feeling? Why was he trying to hide the answers to those questions so desperately from her?

"Look, I know it isn't any of my business…And I know that you and I are just, you know, partners in crime or whatever."

"Sure."

"But why *did* things end between you and Vivienne? I mean, you're obviously eager to get her back and she seems pretty excited to *be* back, but the tabloids made it all seem kind of…"

"A big mess?"

"Exactly."

She hadn't wanted to say, but, yes, that's how it looked from the outside. The gossip sites and the tabloids and the Instagram newsfeed that Annie had helped her curate told a story of betrayal and heartbreak, but one that included way more accusations and speculations than hard facts. Rose sipped her coffee to try and calm her nerves as she waited for Cole to answer her question.

She waited for him to finally tell her the truth.

"So, Vivienne and I…Vivienne is a very pragmatic woman. She's not the romantic type. She doesn't want any kind of big fuss made over feelings. She's just very practical and thinks that relationships should be the same way. Relationships, to her, are more like partnerships. Business deals. You find someone you trust to make your life better."

That sounded like he was justifying Vivienne to himself, rather than trying to explain the particulars of a person he loved. Not that it was any of Rose's business.

"But…?"

She sensed that there was one of those coming on. She was right.

"But I didn't really realize that until she broke up with me."

"What do you mean?"

Cole's eyes took on the far-off gaze of someone recounting the worst memory of their life as if through a thick pane of glass. As if the story had happened to someone else and he was just retelling it for posterity.

"I mean that when we first started dating, I understood that she was very business-minded and serious about stuff like publicity. But when it came to the romance stuff, I thought she was just, you know, a little bit guarded. Like she needed some help coming out of her shell and accepting a little bit of romance or whatever. I thought I would be her knight in shining armor, the one who could open her up to a whole new world of experiences and emotions. I thought I could change her. I thought she wanted to change."

Another pause. Rose got the feeling there would be more of these to come. She nudged him gently with her arm.

"...But?" she prompted.

Her eyes glided over in his direction, where she tried to size him up. All at once, he was guarded, but seemed slightly relieved to be saying these words out loud. She wondered if he'd ever told anyone this story before, or if this was the first time he'd managed to confess the truth.

"But then, I quit *Crime Spree: Beach City*. I didn't tell anyone I was going to do it. I was so fed up with the whole thing, I wanted to make a change, and I knew everyone was going to try and talk me out of it. For once, I just wanted to make my own decisions without everyone trying to change my mind."

"I know the feeling," she said, offering him a small smile of camaraderie.

"And when I came home after telling the network that I was done, she was...inconsolable. Tried to get me to go back and tell them I'd stay on with the show, tried everything to get me to take it back. When I told her I wasn't going to do that, she was fine for a few weeks. Or, she seemed fine, anyway."

Rose's blood rushed in her ears. She didn't like the way this story was going.

"And then?"

"And then, I found out that she wasn't really fine. She was actually seeing my co-star. And then, when I found out about that—through a tabloid—she officially broke up with me. She told me that she couldn't be with someone throwing away their career and their future. That Tyson had *more promise*."

It all made sense now. His reticence to tell anyone the truth. His attempts to win her back. His dedication to this role and the importance he placed on succeeding with it. If this movie was a success, then it would mean she had been wrong. That he *was* more than just his television role, his social media engagement and a pretty face to appear alongside hers in the tabloids.

Rose's heart ached for him. She understood what it was like to carry the weight of people's expectations.

"Oh, I see. Now that it looks like you have a future and a career again…"

"She's back. But you know, things might be different. *She* could be different."

Doubt filled Rose at that statement. But she wasn't going to dash his dreams. Not when they clearly meant so much to him.

"I'm sure she will be, Cole. Don't worry."

A few hours later, Rose was back at work, trying to drown her thoughts of Cole and Vivienne in the scent of fresh flowers she was preparing for May's upcoming engagement party tomorrow. But she should have known that, like where there was smoke, there was fire, so too where there was drama, there was Annie Martin. The woman arrived in a whirlwind of expensive fabric and her usual oversized sunglasses.

Strange how the pictures of Vivienne in Rose's head and Annie Martin were so similar. On the surface, they were both shallow big-city types, obsessed with appearances and image; but they couldn't have been more different underneath.

"Hey, Annie," Rose said, almost immediately returning to her work.

"*Hey, Annie?* Don't you *hey, Annie* me, young lady."

"I'm older than you."

"Doesn't matter. What does matter is…" High-heeled steps carried Annie straight to the counter, where she leaned in as though she had a great secret to divulge and didn't want anyone else in the completely empty store to overhear. "Have you heard the news?"

"That my favorite Giants player is going to become a free agent next season?" Rose deadpanned. "Yes, I'm heartbroken."

"You know that's not what I meant," Annie hissed.

"What did you mean, then?"

"Cole McKittrick's ex-girlfriend—"

"Oh, my stars, what an absolutely *darling* little place."

The ending to Annie's sentence had, undoubtedly, been *is here*, but even she couldn't have predicted how right she was. Because the woman herself was there, standing in the doorway of Rose's shop. In all of her runaway glory—perfect blonde hair blowing in the air conditioning breeze. Perfect, tanned legs glowing even in the fluorescent lights of the shop.

Looking just as perfect as Cole deserved.

"Hi, can I help you?"

"I don't know. Are you Rose Anderson?"

The hairs on the back of her neck rose on end. So, this was the infamous Vivienne. The one who'd made Cole feel as if he was unworthy for daring to take a risk. The one who only thought he was worth something when his name came early in the credits. Rose forced her smile.

"Mm-hm. Town florist. At your service. Is there something I can do to help you, miss?"

"Oh, that is so cute. I can't remember the last time I went somewhere someone didn't know my name. But I'm sure you all are too busy out here to keep up with gossip."

That's when Vivienne supposedly "noticed" Annie. Rose doubted her sincerity.

"Annie? Annie Martin! Yes, I'd heard you moved out to the sticks. Absolutely charming. How have you been?"

Annie opened her mouth to speak, but Rose could already predict what was coming out next. "Better than you," she would have said, and the last thing Rose needed right now was a catfight in her shop.

"Annie's just helping me out today," she said, attempting to avert disaster. "She's got a great eye for color. Is there something we can do for you?"

"Yes, actually. I thought maybe I could talk to you. In private. Maybe we could create an arrangement together?"

With easy motion, Vivienne reached for one of the florist's baskets on the floor and tucked it into the crook of her arm. The action gave Rose just enough time to realize that she didn't really have a choice in the matter, not if she wanted to at least attempt to uphold her veneer of politeness.

"Sure. Annie, do you mind running down to Talley's and checking on my book order?"

"Yeah. Fine."

Of course, Annie Martin didn't go gracefully or tactfully. She left, shooting daggers at Vivienne the whole way. She also managed to slam the door behind her. Vivienne, to her credit, didn't even jump in surprise or return Annie's glare; she simply strolled the shop with her basket and her skirt flaring out all around her, giving the appearance that she was floating along on a cloud instead of walking across solid ground in dizzying high heels.

"Annie has always been a little high-strung. Must be difficult to be in such a close, confined space with her. She and I could barely share Los Angeles; I'm shocked she shares Hillsboro with anyone."

"Annie's a good friend," Rose said, noncommittally.

"Good friend. Hard to come by these days, don't you think?"

"I guess that all depends."

"You're right. Because, you see, I'm a good friend to Cole McKittrick."

"Oh, right. Yes, I think I remember now. I might have read something about you in the newspaper."

It was a low blow, implying that Cole hadn't ever talked about Vivienne or mentioned her name. Rose didn't usually like taking cheap shots—the thing about cheap shots was that they usually left the shooter feeling as cheap as the target—but this time, she couldn't resist.

It was wrong. But for a moment, she relished that wrongness. She wanted someone to hurt as much as she did.

Swallowing back the urge, she promised herself she wouldn't do it again. Just because Cole loved this woman instead of her…that didn't mean she had any right to try and tear her down.

"Yes, well. Cole is such a hard-working guy. You have to know how hard he's worked for his career, for his livelihood."

"Yeah, I know. He's told me."

"It's just…" Vivienne glanced across the small shop from under thick, heavy, impossibly long eyelashes. "I've seen *your* picture in the paper, too."

Rose tried not to let this news affect her. "I hope they got my good side."

"And I have to say…You and Cole haven't known each other very long, which means you might not *really* know him. Might not really know what he wants. Things may seem bright and easy right now because you're having this whirlwind romance but believe me… Cole has almost always put his career first. You seem like a really, really nice girl. I just don't want to see you get hurt."

"I don't think Cole would hurt me. He's not the kind of guy who would do that."

In the silence that followed that declaration, Rose was surprised to discover that it was the truth. Her heart told her that Cole *was* worthy of her trust. She'd been burned before, and she'd been careful not to let anyone get too close. But Cole had worked his way into her heart, and earned the trust she'd sworn never to give anyone ever again.

Vivienne, on the other hand, didn't seem sure. Her wide, sympathetic eyes didn't seem to hold any hint of deception in them, not even as she took the flowers from Rose's counter and slid a handful of bills across in exchange. There was a hint of sadness in her voice, as if she was disappointed to be the bearer of bad news.

"Us Hollywood types…We're all phony in one way or another. Today, he might seem like the nicest guy, the one who would never break your heart. But in a few weeks? When this whole film shoot is over and he has to go back to L.A.?"

She left the question hanging, but Rose did not pick it up.

"I just worry that perhaps Cole isn't the man you think he is. That maybe you don't know the whole story about him."

"What don't I know?"

A secret, infuriating smile came across Vivienne's lips. "Oh, that's not my secret to tell."

With a small shake of her head, she sent a wave of expensive, freesia-scented shampoo in Rose's direction before turning to leave.

"Just think about it, alright?"

And Rose did. Within seconds, the woman disappeared through the front door, leaving Rose with a million more questions than she'd had before she'd entered.

No. That wasn't even true. Rose knew exactly what she had to do, knew exactly what her heart and her gut and every other part of her was telling her. The problem was her stubborn feelings. They all wanted her to run straight to Cole, throw caution to the wind, and demand to know exactly what he was hiding so she could just confess her own feelings.

Moments later, once the coast was well and truly clear, Annie appeared back in the shop with that patented look of lowered-sunglasses concern she had perfected over the course of their friendship.

Rose busied herself with a tricky roll of receipt paper; anything to avoid the weight of her friend's stare.

"Rose? Rose, are you okay?"

"Me?" she replied, too breathless and pitched too high. "Oh, yeah. Sure."

"What did *she* have to say to you?"

On this point, Rose didn't need to lie or conceal the truth. After all, as calculating and sharp-elbowed as Vivienne may have seemed at first, she had offered Rose some valuable information. Not much of it, but enough.

Rose faked a smile as best she could when it felt like her heart was about to fall to the floor like snipped, stray thorns on a rose's stem.

"Nothing I didn't need to hear."

Chapter Eighteen

Cole

Cole should have known that, of all the people in the world, Annie Martin would have gotten her hands on the news first.

When he walked back to his hotel that night, head still swimming from the day and its unexpected detours, he spotted her waiting outside of the lobby, hands crossed in front of her chest and disposition decidedly dark and dangerous. From the set of her shoulders—stern and serious—he could tell exactly what she wanted to see him about. It had taken him long enough to stop thinking about Rose and Vivienne and the war raging in his own heart. He'd fought back his feelings for Rose and let his mind decide for him that Vivienne was the best person for him, a difficult decision to say the least. The last thing he needed was Annie's meddling to come in and ruin his carefully cultivated calm. In that exact second, Cole decided that today was an excellent day to try out the back entrance he'd heard so much about.

Too late. He'd been caught. From even as far down the block as he was, he could hear her hissing. She shot her words like daggers across the slightly frosty fall air.

"Ezekiel Andrew Coleman, don't you dare walk away from me!"

Cole's heart stopped. He might have been able to keep walking if she hadn't tossed out *Ezekiel* as easily as his angry mother had back in the day, back before she and his father stopped talking to him for "being seduced by Hollywood" and changing the God-given name they'd graced him with. The sound of that name, a name he hadn't heard in years, shocked him right down to his core. Instead of turning tail and running away from Annie as fast as he could—what he objectively *should* have done—he found himself drawing nearer to her, meeting her under the golden puddles of the hotel's exterior lights.

"How…How did you know?"

"Are you *seriously* worrying about your super-secret fake identity right now?"

"I got my name legally changed years ago. Yes, I'm wondering how the hell you found out."

All of the records containing his old name were supposed to be sealed. Every shrewd manager and business contact had told him that it would be bad for business if people went around knowing that swaggering, handsome Cole McKittrick was *actually* just some guy from hick country called Ezekiel.

In the words of one man, *Ezekiel goes to the movies; Cole stars in them.*

Annie didn't care about Cole's shock. In fact, shock had been her entire goal. She'd wanted to catch him off guard, probably, and she knew that calling him by his birth name would be the best way to go about it.

"Because I know everything, Ezekiel. Including this new development between you and the wicked witch of West Hollywood! What the hell?"

"Did you just swear?"

The surprises just kept coming in this conversation. In Los Angeles, a town that was practically built upon four-letter words, Annie was known for her practiced, performed linguistic purity. "Oh, rats," and "You've got to be kidding me," were the harshest things she ever said.

The only thing keeping him from calling an ambulance to give her a full work-up was Annie's eyes and the determined set of her jaw, which told him she wouldn't be going anywhere until she got whatever it was she came here for.

To chew him out for Vivienne's sudden appearance, presumably.

"Rose is my best friend in the entire world," she said, with all of the ire of someone about to sentence him to a particularly long prison term. "No one has ever looked out for me or cared about me like she has. If I have the power to help her, then you're damn right I'm going to."

Another swear word. Things were getting serious.

But no matter how strongly Annie felt about something, Cole knew one thing to be true. Him and Rose. They weren't Annie's story to live or to micromanage, not hers to interfere in. Rose wanted control over her own life.

"She doesn't want your help, Annie."

"Fine, then. I'm not helping Rose. I'm helping *you*, you double-crossing douch—"

"Hey!"

His protests fell on deaf ears. But at least they weren't talking about his past anymore. Annie flattened her gaze and went into full-on interrogation mode. And while Cole knew he had a million things to do before production started in just three days—memorizing the lines from the new pages he'd been sent this morning, reading the last of Rose's romance novel syllabus, deciding what to do about his growing feelings for her and Vivienne's sudden arrival—he also knew that trying to avoid Annie when she went into this mode of conversation would only end badly.

"What is Vivienne doing in town?"

"She came here to see me," Cole said, shuffling his feet and trying to evade as much as he could.

"And *why* did she come here to see you? Because if you tell me that it's to win you back, then I swear to God, Cole, I'm going to walk in front of the next moving train just so I don't have to watch it happen."

Okay. Fair enough.

Annie cleared her throat. "You aren't saying anything."

"Well, I don't want you to get run over by a train, do I?"

"Oh, you are an impossible man! And I'm *surrounded* by impossible men, so for you to take the cake…that's saying something."

Their voices were rising, but thankfully, the clientele of the hotel was either tucked away safely at the bar or in their hotel rooms, meaning there was no one outside to witness the dressing-down he was receiving. It wasn't like Cole didn't know he was impossible. It wasn't like he didn't realize he was in a sincere jam here, at the apex of this love triangle. He didn't need Annie reminding him of what he'd been agonizing over all day.

"What do you want me to do? Send her home?"

"Yes. Obviously."

Cole tutted and shook his head. Where was the woman who always held an extra party for the waiters and bartenders who'd staffed her charity events? Where was the woman who'd just posted pictures of herself volunteering her weekends on an animal therapy farm? The woman who'd befriended him when everyone in Hollywood just wanted something from him? He assessed her through narrowed eyes. "You have the biggest heart of anyone I know. You can't be nice to Vivienne?"

"I have a big heart for people who have one of their own."

That was a little harsh, though Cole couldn't deny the dark part of him that agreed with her on that count. "*Annie.*"

"You and Rose are meant for each other."

She wasn't going to let it go, was she? She was going to stand here, on the sidewalk, and scream about how they were destined to fall in love until her voice gave out and her fingertips turned blue from the cold. And if Cole didn't tell her the truth, he was going to have to stand here, tormented by what he couldn't have, forever.

"Me and Rose are fake. Okay? We're fake. We aren't dating for real. We've been working on trying to get *you* and her family off of her back, okay? And I've been trying to get some chemistry training before I go into filming. We aren't real. She doesn't want me. She could *never* want me. And that's the end of it, okay?"

He hadn't realized how much keeping that inside had affected him. But by the time the words were out there, unable to be taken back, he let out a long, relaxing sigh, one that made the tense muscles in his shoulders go slack. Out in front of the hotel, there was a small, tasteful porch swing, a quaint touch for anyone waiting for a cab in high heels or waiting for the rest of their party to meet them before walking to dinner. Cole fell into it, relishing the feeling of being off of his feet, of giving up the fight.

Annie just blinked at him.

"Oh, I knew that. About you two being fake? Yeah, me and her sister figured it out ages ago."

What?

"You *knew*?"

Annie shrugged and took the seat next to him on the swing, using the bottoms of her wedge heels to gently rock them back and forth.

"Rose isn't the kind of person who just jumps into a relationship. Based on that fact alone, I knew that something was up."

Cole let that realization sink in. So…Annie knew that their relationship and all of the pieces and parts that the public knew about it were fake. And still she was here, arguing for him to kick Vivienne out of his life and start over with Rose? It didn't make any sense.

"But you still think we're meant for each other?"

"Only because I have eyes," Annie snarked.

"Well, for the first time in your perfect little life, Annie Martin, you're not going to get what you want. We aren't meant for each other because she doesn't want me."

"You haven't told her the truth about you, have you?"

Cole's entire body tensed. "No. No, I haven't."

"That's going to break her heart. She can't stand liars."

"I know," Cole said. "Have you talked to her about this?"

"Not in so many words, but, come on. Everyone has heard about your little stunt in the jailhouse. I haven't brought it up to her, but I know how she feels about you, and it isn't so bad that she wants to hook you up with your little Hollywood hex."

"That wasn't even a very good pun."

"I know. I've run out of steam. The point is that Vivienne isn't the problem here. You are."

Sure enough, Annie's posture had slipped, and she turned to shoot him a piercing, truth-demanding look. Friendly, but serious.

"So, how do you feel about Rose?"

"What do you mean?"

"You went on for quite a while about how she didn't want you, but you didn't say anything about your own feelings. What are they?"

As he struggled to find the words to answer, a handful of cars and cyclists passed in front of the hotel. The mechanical clock inside the hotel chimed the hour. And Cole tried to decide if his feelings were more important than what Rose wanted.

There wasn't even a question in his mind.

"My feelings don't matter now."

"That's ridiculous."

"No, really. They don't." That was what love was, right? Putting your selfish feelings below the person you cared about. And he really, really did care for Rose Anderson. More than he could probably say. "All she wants is control over her own life and her own destiny. She wants someone who won't lie to her, who hasn't lied to her. She made it clear once that she didn't want me. She told me time and time again how she is going to fall in love and it certainly wasn't like this. Not with someone like me. And if I tried to force her hand now, if

I told her now how I feel about her, then it would be like spitting in the face of what she wants. I can't do that to her. It's not fair."

"Or, you could say you're letting her make a huge decision without all of the facts."

He hadn't thought about it that way. Great. Another thing to feel conflicted about.

"I really…She's really…" *She's wonderful. The best thing that's ever happened to me. I am starting to fall in love with her and know I absolutely shouldn't.* It wasn't like he could say any of that to Annie, though. It was hard enough admitting that to himself, much less to her. "I don't have words for my feelings, if I'm being honest. Not yet."

Annie raised one eyebrow. "But you think that things could…"

"I think that I care about her enough to let her make her own choices. And it's clear that she's made her mind up about me. Even if she doesn't know it yet."

They didn't speak for a long time. The gentle swing of their seat lulled his thoughts into calm circles rather than the frenetic hurricanes they'd been just a few moments ago.

"You know you've got to tell her, don't you? You can't go through the rest of your life with an unanswered question that big weighing on your heart."

"A heart? What's that?"

But even as Annie nudged him and rolled her eyes, Cole was beginning to make up his mind. Yes. He would tell her. He would tell her everything.

And then, he would let her make the decision. He would put his heart right in her hands.

He could only hope she wouldn't break it.

Chapter Nineteen

Rose

Rose didn't get nervous at parties. It wasn't like she particularly loved partying or anything like that—Annie was the party animal among their little circle of friends and sisters—but she didn't mind them, either. Parties were, in her estimation, the perfect place for happiness to happen. Good food. Good music. Good friends. Maybe a sip or two of champagne, if she felt like rolling the dice.

But as she got ready for May's engagement party, she could barely put on her lipstick. Her hands rattled and shook, making her color outside the lines against her will.

This was what she and Cole had been working their way towards this entire time. He would be going back to Vivienne and his movie's filming soon, and she finally got through a night without anyone asking her why she was alone. A night where no one would try to set them up with their handsy sons, where she could finally step out from under the shadow of being "poor, pitiful, single Rose Anderson." She should have been ecstatic, and she knew it.

Yet no matter how many times she reminded herself of that fact, the lipstick wouldn't stay in place. Her hands wouldn't stop shaking.

Her mind wouldn't stop replaying that one moment when Vivienne told her that Cole wasn't the man he seemed.

She was in love with him. She wasn't sure when that had happened. Maybe it was when he told her he saw her as no one in town did. Maybe it was his crooked smile and his big heart and the way he felt like he had to hide both. She didn't know why or how it happened. She only knew that it had happened. And tonight, she knew all of that was going to end. It had to, right?

Oh, she was the worst kind of cliché. She'd known from the beginning that fake relationships in the books always ended up with someone falling in love. She'd been so arrogant to think that she could cheat fate.

Somewhere in the midst of this poor lipstick application, her mother's familiar knock sounded on the loft door, and she took the liberty of letting herself in. Annemarie Anderson was already dressed for the party, which was being prepared outside and would take over most of the family's flower farm property. The flowers would be kept safe from any stranger's hands or wandering, but their beauty would be on full display.

In the mirror where Rose was inspecting herself—with her hair swept away from her face, to show off the deep-green dress she'd chosen for the occasion—she saw her mother's sandy eyebrows knit together in concern.

"Darling? Are you alright?"

"Yeah, of course," Rose lied, a fake smile sticking her lips to her teeth. "Why do you ask?"

"It's just that I don't think I've ever seen anyone apply lipstick that poorly, and certainly not you."

Rose's hand froze over her lips. Retiring the lipstick to the vanity, she let out a long, exhausted sigh.

"I'm…" There was no point in hiding the truth. Her mother already knew that she was in love. "I'm having a weird night, Mom."

"It's about that Cole boy, isn't it?"

The hairs on the back of Rose's neck stood on end. This was usually the part of her mother's romance-centric speeches where she waxed poetic about the joys of marriage and how handsome the current man in her daughter's life was. Rose had seen it a thousand times, not just in her own life, but in the lives of her sisters, too.

"His ex-girlfriend came back into town," Rose said, trying to shut down the conversation as quickly and easily as she could. "He thinks they're meant for each other or something. I don't know."

There was a pause. Rose stared at her hands on the vanity instead of back at her mother's reflection.

"But he chose you, didn't he?"

Rose's heart lodged in her throat. He'd never picked her. Not even in the beginning. Their relationship had been fake and convenient and driven entirely by their own needs. It wasn't real love for him, not like it was for her. "I don't know. I don't think so."

Another pause.

"Well, dear. You know I've always wanted you to find love. More than anything."

"Yes, ma'am."

Here we go. Time for the speech about fighting for romance and never giving up. Can't wait.

"When I met your father, I thought I was never going to find it. That feeling you get when you know someone will be there, at your side, forever. He changed my life. Finding love like that changed my life."

"I know. You always say—"

"I'm not finished."

It wasn't an unkind reply, but it was more of a stern refusal than Rose had ever heard her mother make before in her entire life. She immediately turned around from the vanity mirror to face the older woman currently sitting on the edge of her bed.

"Oh. Sorry."

Her mother had always been crazed when it came to romance. All she ever did, it seemed, was focus on her accounting business, indulge in her afternoon gossip sessions with her friends, and push her daughters towards love.

"It's because I went through that that I can say with one hundred percent certainty, that if you don't know if he's chosen you, then you have to choose yourself."

Rose's heart practically stopped. All her life her mother had told her that the key to happiness was love. And now this?

"Mom?"

"If you really love him, then I know that will be hard. But I promise, in the long run, you will be happier."

There was no sign of uncertainty in her mother's eyes. It was all sincere, and perhaps a little bit desperate. She wasn't going to let her daughter make a mistake.

"But you've always said you want us to get married and fall in love and—"

"Because I want you to be happy. You're never going to be happy with a man who doesn't choose you. Trust is the most important thing in any relationship. It's what everything else is built on. If that crumbles…" She trailed off and reached out to take Rose's hand in hers. Her skin was cool and soft as she tightened her grip. "Darling, superficial love is worse than none at all. I promise you that."

How could Rose doubt her?

But strangely, for the first time since she'd kissed Cole, Rose felt…almost okay. Her heart was still aching, but it wasn't anything she couldn't handle.

"Thanks, Mom."

Her mother smiled, wide and warm and maternal. "Now, I want you to have a good time tonight, you hear? Dance and laugh and hang out with your sisters and kiss the poor guy if you want. But don't give him your heart if he isn't worthy of it."

Unbidden tears pooled in Rose's eyes. She could do this. She *would* be okay. "I won't."

"Good. A good heart should never be wasted on someone who doesn't deserve it, my girl. And your tears shouldn't, either."

The engagement party had taken over the entire Anderson Flower Farm—from the refined cocktail party in the rustic barn to the wine tasting station on the front porch, to the dance floor that had been constructed at the top of the hill where the cars usually parked. Annie, as per usual, had gone all out in planning, and Rose couldn't help but smile every time she saw one of her own hand-constructed flower arrangements on a nearby table, or saw someone enjoying the slices of Millie's Pie Joint pie that had been cut, fried, and brought around like dessert canapés on fancy toothpicks.

This was a celebration worthy of Tom and May, two high school sweethearts who'd found each other after years apart, and it was perfect. Just like the conversation she'd had with her mom earlier this evening, the party itself reminded Rose that everything happened for a reason…and love could always be just around the corner.

When she finally found the happy couple—well, her sister's half of it, anyway—she threw her arms around her and pulled her into a tight hug.

"You look beautiful."

"So do you! Positively glowing," May said, raising her eyebrows suggestively. "I've heard a rumor that you're in love."

Rose's stomach twisted. She shouldn't have been surprised that word had reached May even out on the road with her new fiancé (they'd been backpacking upstate since the last time they'd been home, and were due to head to Canada tomorrow once the last bits of the party were cleaned up), but the thought of Cole still sent shockwaves through her.

"It's just a little fling. That's all."

"I don't know," May said, unconvinced. Her eyes then slid just over Rose's shoulder, and her lips curled into a devilish smile. "There's a guy on your six who's looking at you like he wants to marry you on the spot. Doesn't look like a fling to me."

When Rose turned around to follow her eyeline, there he was. Looking perfectly red-carpet ready and billboard handsome in a dark-wash suit. His eyes glowed in the fairy lights strung high above them, and when they met her own, she felt a pang of regret when she remembered that it wasn't real.

At least, it wasn't real for him. He was playing a part with her right now, the public performance of the love-struck boyfriend.

Behind her, she could feel May slip away into the crowd to find Annie and Harper, but she didn't care. She focused on the tall man striding towards her like she was the last woman left on Earth.

"In the novels, this is usually the part where the hero sweeps the heroine into his arms and professes how beautiful she is."

God, he was painfully charming. Rose tried to resist, even as she smiled and played her part, too.

"Well, this isn't a romance novel, is it?"

"No. No, it's not. But do you think I could have this dance anyway?"

Rose practically choked as he offered his hand to her. He'd been here thirty seconds and he already wanted a dance?

"I don't know—"

"Rose. Please." His eyes were swimming with emotions she wanted to believe were sincere. "May I have this dance?"

Once again, he offered her his hand. She knew better than to take it. Taking it would lead to dancing, which was against the rules. Sure, skinny-dipping had also been against the rules, but that had been part of their agenda. This? This felt decidedly different. Romantic. Sexy. Dangerous.

Still…this was probably the last time she'd be this close to him. She couldn't say no. More importantly, she didn't want to.

Carefully, she let him draw her into his arms, where he pressed himself against her and she allowed her body to melt against his. The makeshift dance floor was full of swaying couples, and all around them, the lyrical swell of the song was growing in passion and intensity, just like the sensations building up within Rose at every point where Cole touched her.

She was electric. Her entire being hummed at his contact, torn between what she wanted and everything she knew she couldn't have. This was their kiss all over again. This was the pond, but worse.

Worse because she knew everything had to end tonight. No matter how charming and lovable he was; no matter how she felt about him.

No matter that their lips were hovering so close now. No matter that she knew he wanted to kiss her. And she wanted to kiss him right back.

He hadn't chosen her. So, she needed to choose herself.

"Rose?" Cole asked, his eyes never leaving hers.

"Yes?"

"Remember what you told me when we first started working together, when we were first watching those black-and-white movies?"

"Mm-hm. *Actions speak louder than words*. It's the, uh, it's the number one rule of romantic chemistry."

She didn't even get to finish the sentence before his lips were upon her own and he drew her in closer, almost immediately deepening their contact. Rose melted. She'd been homesick for kissing him since the second she stopped last time, and all she wanted was this. This closeness, this feeling. His hand on her cheek and his heartbeat against her own and—

And if she kept kissing him, she knew she was never going to be able to stop. No matter how wrong it was.

With all of her strength, she pulled away. Breathless. Heart racing.

She didn't care that there were people all around them. She didn't care that there were wondering eyes certainly looking in their direction. She stopped swaying. Stopped dancing. Stopped moving.

For a long moment, neither of them spoke. Cole, apparently, was waiting on her to break the ice, but it took her a while before she was able to break free from the haze.

"I…" she said, still fighting to catch her breath. She couldn't look at him. Couldn't brave facing him like this. "I shouldn't have done that."

Chapter Twenty

Cole

I shouldn't have done that. That might have been the world's most tragic collection of words ever to follow such a life-changing kiss.

When she pulled away from him that had been the last thing he'd been expecting to hear from her. After all, he'd felt something during that kiss—mostly that he didn't want it to end. Surely, she must have felt the same thing, must have tasted in that kiss everything he'd been unable to say out loud? *I shouldn't have done that* didn't sound anything like the *I love you, too* he'd been dreaming of.

It took a moment before he managed to catch his breath and compose his thoughts into actual words. Blinking at her, he searched her face for any hint or indication that he was hallucinating, that this was all a big joke and eventually, she would laugh and confess that she'd truly loved him this whole time. When he didn't find any, he asked:

"Maybe we should get off the dance floor, hm?"

Wordlessly agreeing, she led him to the back of the barn, where the chaos of the party melted into dark solitude. They could hear the party, of course, and see its glow, but here in the shadows, they could at least pretend they were alone.

At the same time that he asked, "What do you mean, you shouldn't have done that," Rose spluttered out, "*Why* did you kiss me?"

Cole's better instincts told him that only heartbreak could come from telling her the truth, but he *needed* her to know. And besides, no one without at least a little bit of love in their heart kissed like that. She hadn't just pressed her lips to his; she'd leaned in, deepened the motion and drawn him deeper into her. It wasn't just physical; it was spiritual, too.

If she kissed him like that, she had to care about him. Maybe it was enough to forgive him.

"I kissed you because I wanted to," he said. Tonight was supposed to be about honesty, so that's what he was going to give her. "I kissed you because I think it's time for us to be honest with each other. To tell the truth."

Rose swallowed, hard. He watched as she struggled to breathe. "The truth?"

He noticed that it was the truth part that caused her eyes to flash and her breathing to become ragged, not the revelation that he wanted to kiss her.

He didn't understand her. Didn't understand why she wouldn't look at him now and why she hadn't wanted to kiss him.

They were both here. They both *clearly* felt something for each other. He could see that in her eyes now. Why was she running away?

Why was she *always* running away? He noticed that about her. For someone who stayed in the same place her entire life, she sure seemed to be running away from a lot of things. From her past. From her choices. From her feelings.

"I…" *I want to know if you think you could love me. I want you to know that I feel something for you, that in only two weeks you've completely rewritten my mental definition of that word.* That was what he'd come here to say, but his mind was still stuck on her. Not her feelings for him, not all of the unfinished business between them. *Her.* "Why are you still living at home?"

"*What?*"

Now that he'd started, he couldn't stop. There were too many unanswered questions playing on his mind. She didn't make sense. Here she was, a strong, creative, beautiful, smart, independent woman with a heart of gold, and yet she was still living at home, hiding away some of her most precious talents.

"And why don't you sell your perfumes? I've smelled some of the scents you've made and they're incredible. Why aren't you doing that?"

A wry, almost shocked laugh burst out of Rose's mouth.

"Oh, when you said you wanted the truth, you meant *my* truth. Not yours."

There was an indignance to her voice he didn't quite understand, but he wasn't going to let that stop him.

"No, we can—"

She rolled her eyes and continued, trampling over whatever it was he thought he was going to say. "Why do you even want to know? So you can have the upper hand here? Or so you can compare me to Vivienne?"

"Rose, I just kissed you. You can't pretend not to feel what I'm feeling. You have to know that I…" He trailed off, trying to channel a little bit of that romcom movie magic. When he came up short, he thought back to the books he'd been reading, searching for anything that could help him navigate this situation. He couldn't lose her. Not now. She needed to know how he felt. "This is the part of the romance novel where we kiss and confess our feelings and ride off into the sunset and live happily ever after."

But this was clearly not what Rose wanted to hear. A fire lit inside of her eyes, nearly hot enough to scald Cole even from a distance.

"No, Cole. This isn't a romance novel. There isn't going to be an *us*. There isn't going to be anything more between us. I live at home because it's all I can afford right now. I can't pursue the perfume thing—which I love—because every time I think about it, I think about the guy who broke my heart and betrayed me. I think about how humiliated I was when he said my dreams were stupid, how entangled this dream was with him. I'm not a heroine. You're not a hero. This isn't a romance novel. And tomorrow, when you go back to Vivienne, that will be *your* happily ever after. There isn't one for us."

He staggered back like he'd been shot. Blindly holding onto the wood paneling beside him for support, he tried his best to recover from what she'd just said.

"But why does it have to be that way?"

"Because you're not real. None of this is real."

He flinched. A wave of indignation surged through him.

"What are you talking about? Sure, we started this thing out all wrong, but just because it wasn't real at the start doesn't mean—"

"Vivienne told me you aren't what you seem."

Cole's voice died in his throat. Oh, no. Vivienne had gotten to Rose first. After a moment of silence, Rose continued.

"She said you're lying to me. And considering you're an actor who basically lies for a living, a guy who doesn't share anything about his past with the people who care about him, I believe her."

"You can't believe everything Vivienne—"

A hand rose to silence him.

"She's not the only one who told me that."

"Who else?"

"Doesn't matter." She shook her head. Her eyes lowered. He had to wonder if she was holding back tears, or if that was just him. "You didn't deny it."

"Rose."

He said her name before realizing he didn't have anything *else* to say. Rose stared back at him, unflinching. He could tell from the defiant set of her chin that she wasn't interested in his pity. She was interested in answers.

"So, tell me, Cole. What's your secret? What have you been lying to me about this whole time?"

His stomach twisted. Yes, he'd promised himself—and Annie— that he would give Rose all the answers she needed about him. He'd thought that she would understand, that she would say she loved him anyway and was glad that they were both honest with each other now.

But he could tell that wasn't going to be the way this shook out. If he told the truth, he was going to lose her. If he *didn't* confess everything, he was going to lose her, too. He tried to delay the inevitable as long as he could.

"I was going to tell you tonight."

"Good news. Tonight is right now. This very minute. You can tell me whenever you're ready."

She folded her arms across her chest in a defensive posture, waiting.

All of a sudden, Cole felt crushing guilt resting upon his shoulders. He'd been able to convince himself for years that his old life was irrelevant. But he was done hiding now. His future happiness depended upon him spilling all his secrets to Rose. And hoping she would forgive him.

"My name isn't Cole McKittrick. It's Ezekiel Andrew Coleman. My name is fake. My entire bio online, too. Cole McKittrick isn't, you know, real. Ezekiel Andrew Coleman, a nobody from nowhere, wasn't going to be famous, so I became…" He pointed at himself, sweeping his hand up and down. "This."

That was the God's honest truth. He'd been Cole for so long that he'd forgotten who he used to be. He'd forgotten that he had a whole other version of himself buried somewhere out in the desert, hidden from the world.

That's why his parents never spoke to him. That's why they'd blocked his numbers. That's why they'd returned every Christmas and birthday and mother's and father's day gift he'd ever sent. That's why they turned the lights off and pretended they weren't home any time he went there. Because he'd changed his name and his life story. Like he was ashamed of where he came from. That's why he needed Vivienne. To legitimize this cool guy image he'd built for himself.

He didn't feel like a fake. But he knew that's what he was. And worse, he knew that's how Rose would see him now.

Her jaw hung open. She blinked. She exhaled, slow and ragged. But she didn't speak. He could almost imagine her running through her mental Rolodex of memories, all the way back to her time with the catfishing guy who'd screwed her over.

"So…" she said, her voice breaking. "You knew from the beginning how that would make me feel."

"Yes, but—"

The tears still didn't fall, not even when she narrowed her eyes and set the full force of her anger directly at him.

"You knew my history. You knew what that jerk had done to me, and you still made me fall in love with you while doing the exact same thing?"

"My feelings for you—"

She let out a sharp bark of a laugh. His heart plummeted.

"You're lucky to still have those, Cole. Because I'm going to be honest. I don't feel anything for you anymore. Honestly, I don't even *know* you anymore."

Without another word and without giving him a second to recover from the verbal blow she'd just thrown at him, she turned on her heel to leave.

"Where are you going?"

"Back to the party. Alone."

"But—"

She turned back again. In that instant, he realized that this would probably be the last time he ever saw her. Desperately, he drank in the details of her face, trying to commit them to memory, trying to hold on to her as long as possible. He only wished that their last shared glance wasn't one filled with so much contempt.

"Listen. Go back to Vivienne. You're right. You both deserve each other."

Chapter Twenty-One

Rose

Rose was true to her word. She *did* rejoin the party, and when she did so, she did it with all of the pretending she could possibly muster. She laughed at all of the jokes and served champagne and helped guests find their way to one of the many buffets scattered around the party. She did the "bride's family" thing and talked to folks from about town who remembered her and her sisters when they were *this tall*.

She even endured the questions about her date and where he'd gone. She repeated her rote answers whenever someone asked her about her love life and her plans for marriage. Over and over and over again.

And eventually, finally, when all of the guests had gone and clean up for the night was over, she took her customary slice of pie and made her way out to the deck, not even bothering to tell her family where she was going. A slice of pie under the stars always seemed to put the world into perspective for her. Always seemed to help her sort the puzzle pieces of her life into a picture she could understand. If there was ever a night when she needed the clarity of the front porch, it was tonight.

It was a beautiful night, an almost sarcastically beautiful night. Not a cloud in the inky dark sky. A full moon that bathed the landscape in cold, soft light. Everything glowed; it would have been the perfect night to fall in love. But Rose tried to look on the bright side, tried to see the good in it. Tonight wasn't the ending of something. No, tonight was the beginning of something. That's why the sky was so clear and so full of stars. The beautiful night was celebrating the start of her new life, of her new journey towards happiness and independence and…

Okay. Maybe she was telling herself a few too many lies tonight. She was so sick of lies.

As she sat there with her thoughts and her pie, which tasted more like dust in her mouth than butter, sugar, and berries, she could slowly sense the presence of her family as, one by one, they stepped cautiously out onto the wooden deck to check on her.

Usually, they all came out here for dessert. Tonight, Rose had gotten a head start without them.

Harper, it turned out, was the only one brave enough to step forward and actually talk to her. Coming up around the back of her seat, Harper took the one beside it and leaned back. They sat in silence for a moment, eating their pie and staring at the stars, catching the scent of the flowers and the trees from far down below as the wind blew up towards them.

The quiet didn't last.

"Do you…" Harper paused, barely glancing up. "Do you want to talk about it?"

"Nope. Sure don't."

Harper didn't say anything. And for once, in Rose's overly micromanaged life, no one questioned her. Instead, her family slowly joined her on the porch, took their seats, and just sat there and ate their pie in silence.

None of them even mentioned it when fresh, hot waves of tears started to slip down Rose's cheeks, catching the moonlight as they tumbled down.

Chapter Twenty-Two

Cole

First days on set were kind of like first days of school. You'd spend so much time preparing for the day, thinking about it, worrying about it, even losing sleep over it, and once it finally arrived, most of it disappeared in a blur of first greetings, new locales and names it would take you weeks to remember. By now, Cole was used to the experience and usually managed to do a good job of putting on a brave and engaged face. He wrote down names when they were given to him so he would remember. He walked the route from his trailer to set as many times as he could to learn the way. He thanked everyone earnestly for their hard work and tried to assure them, without ever saying the words aloud, that he would do his best to make the experience as professional and fun as he possibly could.

Today, though? Today, he walked through with all of the strength and presence of a ghost. Six a.m. wake-up call. Vivienne met him in the lobby of the hotel and promptly replaced the homemade muffin from the bakery down the street and his hot chocolate with a black coffee and an aspirin. He took both and allowed the handler from the studio to lead them to the car that would bring them both to set. It was only around the corner, but insurance dictated the measure. He didn't mind. The drive, short as it was, gave him time to think about Rose.

That was the problem. The whole morning, he ended up thinking about Rose. She was the haze in front of his eyes, the one that cast a shadow over every smile he forced, every despondent word he spoke and every lackluster handshake he offered. They were so close to her shop, filming just down the street. If he craned his neck out of the window of his trailer he was sure he would have been able to see the cute, painted letters of the windows and the orchids attempting to crawl up towards the sun.

He forced himself to stay in his trailer. Forced himself not to go and wander that short distance to check in on the flowers in the window or to make sure that she'd remembered to turn off all but the emergency lights, a part of her evening routine she frequently forgot when she was wrapped up in a good audiobook or was thinking about her latest shipment.

She wouldn't want to see him anyway. And after spending so long bending her rules, Cole would finally do the right thing and obey her wishes.

He let himself be dragged around like a rag doll on the set, encouraged by the petite, stunning blonde on his arm. Vivienne smiled and crooned and said all of the right things and took selfies and pictures of the oh-so quaint little town at all of the perfect angles. They got him into hair. Into makeup. Into wardrobe. Eventually, he found himself alone in his trailer, in a blessed moment of quiet peace.

His mind, though, wasn't quiet. He kept going back to the night before, back to Rose. Back to what she'd said. About how she'd made him feel. An emptiness filled his chest, and one thought filled his mind.

I miss my parents.

When they'd stopped talking to him, after he'd changed his name and almost everything else about him—which they saw as him disowning them, disowning his own life—he'd shut off the part of his heart that thought too much about them. He'd forgotten what it was like to feel really loved, to know the simple joy of a hug from someone who cared about you.

He'd felt that again with Rose. And now he'd lost it. All he wanted to do was feel it again.

His pride told him to resist. His mind told him it was a terrible idea. But when he looked around his trailer and saw a telephone hooked into the wall, he walked over and dialed the familiar number.

It rang twice. An eternity. And then, a small, feminine voice popped up.

"Coleman residence."

His heart raced.

"Uh…Mom?"

"Ezekiel?"

"Yeah, it's me."

A pause. A sigh. He could almost envision her sinking into the small stool beside the wall-mounted phone in the kitchen.

"I haven't heard you answer to that name in a long time."

"Haven't heard anyone use it in a long time. It's…it's good to hear your voice."

"Yours too, son."

Son. It wasn't much. But it was a start.

They talked for a while longer after that. Awkward. Stilted. But it was the most important conversation he'd had in a long, long time.

It was a step towards remembering who he was. Towards being honest with himself. About himself. About his past. About the man he wanted to be.

He'd always been bad at that, hadn't he? He'd lied to himself about his life, lied to himself about his feelings for Vivienne, lied to himself about his feelings for Rose. It was in this state that he allowed himself to be led out at last for filming. They pushed him out into the street scene, where he was supposed to have his first big moment with his on-screen love interest.

That was the reason Vivienne was here, of course, sitting in a nearby chair as she scrolled through her phone. This morning, when she'd seen the call sheet and met him in the lobby with coffee, she'd insisted on accompanying him "for inspiration." He'd laughed and smiled at the time, offering a good, convincing performance of the perfect, almost-once-again boyfriend.

But as the takes rolled by, it was clear that her "inspiration" wasn't working. And by take fifteen, the morale of the crew and the assembled staff dipped low. Fiona Marks, his co-star, shifted on the balls of her feet, her expression darkening and twisting into a sour pout every time their director, Lawrence, yelled cut.

Dammit. Damn it all.

He just couldn't get it right, he was so distracted. His head was in a thousand different places and none of them were the depths of his co-star's eyes, lovely as they were. Every time his mind wandered to thoughts of romance, memories of Rose flooded in which then, in turn, made him angry at himself.

What do I want? Am I being honest with myself?

Apparently, though, Fiona couldn't handle this latest cut to her love scene. Ripping at her jacket, fighting her way out of the sleeves, Fiona leveled her piercing eyes in his direction.

"You know, man, what's your deal?"

"My deal?" he parroted.

"You haven't been yourself all morning. Just clear your head and *act*, man."

"That's the problem. I can't clear my head."

And I can't seem to be myself, either.

"Then focus on something else. Focus on anything that'll wrap up this scene and get me out of these damn heels, alright?"

In the short break in production while their director went to chat with the director of photography and the makeup assistant came to give Cole a slight touch-up on his forehead shine, his mind wandered again. This time to last night, and the woman he'd spent it with.

He thought about his phone call with his mother, and how rejected he'd always felt when he thought of his parents. He thought of all the sacrifices he'd made to become Cole McKittrick. Of all the pieces and parts of himself he'd buried, just for a shot at fame and notoriety.

His eyes refocused over his co-star, Fiona Marks's shoulders, where Vivienne was sitting with a water bottle full of green juice in one hand and her illuminated cell phone screen in the other.

He needed to be honest with himself. Was Vivienne *really* his Person? Or was he just choosing her because she was what the tabloids wanted? Was he really letting them control his entire life, even who he decided to love? Was he really going to let them write his story?

For so long, he'd let his own identity slip through his fingers. He'd allowed himself to lose control of his own life. Maybe it was time to take it back. Maybe it was time to start remembering who he was. And that started here. Right now.

Extracting himself from the makeup girls with a sudden, frightening urgency, he made a beeline for the short, squat fair-haired man currently in deep conversation with the woman checking lighting levels and adjusting her camera accordingly. Cole waited until he could get a word in edgewise.

"Lawrence, can I take ten?"

At the sound of his voice, Lawrence's slightly balding head popped up, clearly torn between coddling his star and giving him an earful.

"Kid, take an hour. I'm going to get some exteriors and give the crew a break while you're gone. Maybe when you come back, you'll have your head on straight, alright?"

"I will. I promise."

Making a beeline straight for his girlfriend sitting at the edge of the live set, Cole cleared his throat and asked the question that had been dancing on the tip of his tongue. Word vomit followed.

"Vivienne, how do you feel about me?"

The woman in question barely glanced up from her phone.

"Feel about you? Cole, what is this about?"

This is about the fact that, for years, I became someone I wasn't. I traded in myself for a chance at fame.

It took all of the strength he possessed—and all of the acting talent that had been noticeably out of his grasp only a moment ago—to keep his tone light and jovial, almost teasing. Vivienne wasn't the kind of woman who talked too much about emotions; he didn't want to scare her off, even if he *needed* to know her answer to this.

She was part of that old life. She was part of the trades and deals he'd made for a new existence. She'd been the *center* of Cole McKittrick's life. If he could let her go, then he could let it all go, too.

"Come on, it's a simple enough question. How do you feel about me?"

"I like you, Cole, and we make a great team."

Wrong answer. It was the answer that Cole himself had given just the night before, but it was still so very, very wrong. Hearing it echoed back to him by the woman he'd thought he loved—the woman with the blank eyes and the cold hands that reached out and patted his own without affection, much less without those sparks he felt every time Rose touched him—shattered any illusions he might have had.

He didn't want a teammate. He didn't want someone to share an image with, didn't want someone who only wanted his company when it would be broadcasted all over the internet. He wanted love.

He wanted someone to love and someone to love him right back. Desperation made him clasp her one hand in his, holding it close as he bent to meet her eyes and beg her to say the right things. To make him believe the right things.

And it was as clear as day to him now that Vivienne would never be her. In fact, even if she *did* want those things, she would still never be the woman he wanted to share them with. Only that meant…that meant that he'd given his soulmate up. He'd lost her.

"I don't know what you expect me to say."

"Say? If you want to be with me, I want you to tell me everything. Tell me I make your heart beat faster or that you're crazy about me or you can't live without me or that every day we were apart was the biggest mistake of your life."

She pulled her hand away as if he'd bitten it. "What has gotten into you?"

"I just need to know. Why did you come out here? Do you really love me?"

There was a time when he would have taken crumbs of affection from her. He'd wanted the relationship to be real for so long, that even if she'd just kissed him and told him they would talk about it after work with a bottle of wine, then he probably would have fallen for it.

…Or would he? Would he have had more of a backbone than that? Had his time with Rose made him a better man?

Well, he'd never find out. Because Vivienne couldn't even give him crumbs.

"Cole, you and I make sense."

"That's not the same as love."

"No, but sometimes it's more important."

For a split second, Cole tried to imagine it. A life without love. Without the consuming, all-powerful love that Rose so often talked about. Without ever again feeling the little firecracker sparks that spread across his skin when she touched him. Going thousands upon thousands of days without her smile or her laughter or the way she looked at him when he was annoying the hell out of her.

A lifetime without the person who made him feel complete.

"Nothing is more important than love," he whispered, trying to get Vivienne to see it.

A few months ago, he wouldn't have believed that. He certainly wouldn't have said it. But now, after reconnecting with his family—tenuous as the beginning might have been—the words rested on his heart, a truth as basic and universal as the blue sky or the green grass.

Vivienne scoffed, her eyes piercing. "When did you start believing that old line?"

There was something about the way she asked that question. The little shake of her head. The smirk that seemed to communicate something like *come on, we both know that stuff is ridiculous.* The way she peered up at him condescendingly from over the tops of her expensive sunglasses. It reminded him of something else Rose had told him once, all the way back when they'd had their first romcom movie night. *Finding your Person is about finding someone who is going to let your true self out, not hide them away.*

But that was what Vivienne had done. Over the time they'd been together, she'd asked him to hide pieces of himself, bit by bit. First, away from the cameras, then, away from her, and finally, away from himself. He wasn't a devil-may-care movie star who cared about media exposure and social media engagement. He was a romantic who believed in breakfast and books, in nights under the stars, in movie marathons and long conversations and afternoon jailbreaks.

And...and...if he stayed with Vivienne, not only was he *not* going to be happy...he wasn't going to be himself. Maybe it would take months, maybe it would take years, but eventually, someday, he would look in the mirror and see a stranger staring back at him.

As this rush of realization crashed over him, he vaguely heard the voice of his co-star call over his shoulder.

"Cole? Do you want to rehearse while we wait?"

All around him, he could feel the expectations of others piling up on his shoulders, threatening to drag him down with them. He had only a moment to make his decision, but once he made it, he knew he wasn't ever going to look back.

Really, it wasn't even a decision. Something in him was always destined for Rose, always meant to run to her. Now, he was going to make that inevitability a reality. His heart felt instantly lighter. He'd read about this moment before in dozens of Rose's romance novels, and the writers had gotten it right. It was like all of the puzzle pieces scattered around the table of his life had suddenly fallen into place, showing him a perfect picture of a future he couldn't wait to get to.

"No. No, I'm sorry. I'm really sorry," he said, ostensibly to answer his co-star's question, though he never let his eyes leave Vivienne's. "But I have to go."

"*What?*"

Her screech cut across the film set, drawing attention to their little corner of drama. Cole bent down, took her hand in his, and tried to make her understand what it had taken him so long to.

"Vivienne, you're such an ambitious, brilliant woman. And you are going to find the man for you someday. I'm just…I'm not him." With that simple declaration, months of pent-up tension and anxiety were released from within the prison of his chest. He'd been fighting to keep exactly the wrong person with him, when all the time, the right one was just by his side, waiting for him to open his heart. Waiting for him to tell the truth and be himself.

"My Person *is* out there. I broke her heart. And now, I've got to do whatever I can to win her back. I'm so sorry, but this is the right thing. For both of us."

And then, he was gone. Running down the street that would bring him to Rose Anderson…and hopefully, towards his happily ever after.

Chapter Twenty-Three

Rose

Rose was doing a very good job of pretending. Pretending she was happy. Pretending she didn't care. Pretending that she couldn't see, from her own shop window, the hotel where the man she loved was probably kissing his very beautiful girlfriend.

That's why she'd decided to close the shop for the day. As good as she was at keeping the pretense up in private, trying to keep her mask on in public was going to be impossible. After all, she wasn't the actor in the relationship. And she'd never been particularly good at lying to anyone except herself.

Cole hadn't taught her how to be a good liar.

The other reason she closed her shop was even more personal and selfish than that. This always happened when she was emotional, when she let her own feelings get wildly out of control. Inspiration for her perfumes always struck, creativity always flowed out of her when she was at her most wild and untethered. If there were tears burning at the back of her throat or gratitude growing so big in her chest that she could hardly hold it, then it was only a matter of time before she had to pour those feelings out into a new, bespoke scent.

Today, the scents pouring out of her were dark and musky, like the corners of her heart where she'd been hiding her true feelings, but they were all equally paired with the notes of things that made her happy. The smell of a wood-burning campfire. The crisp snap of fall wind. It smelled like heartbreak *and* healing, all in the same breath. Even at her worst, the sunshine tried to glow through her internal gloom, and that, at least, made her smile a little bit.

Not much. But as the familiar smells of warmth, happiness and comfort even in the worst of times started to wrap around her like a familiar winter coat, that little bit was enough.

It was a start. And for Rose, who had gone to bed crying and whose heart still ached, a start was all she needed. A little light at the end of the tunnel for her to follow.

She would get through this. She had to.

"Knock, knock."

Rose's heart stopped. Her hands froze over the two beakers she'd been inspecting, trying to decide between them for her next scent note in the perfume of her feelings.

It couldn't be. Forcing herself to speak, she tried, in vain, to force her voice to sound somewhat normal, and not like the strangled warble it came out as.

"Who is it?"

"Probably someone you don't want to see."

No denying it now. That was Cole McKittrick on the other side of her workshop door. Of all the people in the world she wanted to see right now, he was the one she wanted most.

And least.

Carefully setting her instruments down, she moved towards the door, barely able to pick up her protesting feet because of the heaviness in her heart weighing them down. A million questions came to the forefront of her mind, demanding her attention. Why is he here? What does he want? Isn't he supposed to be filming a movie today? Why can't he just get out of my life? Do I even want to see him again? But only one question made it to her lips.

"Cole?"

There was a small curtained window built into the door of her little workshop, a precious detail her father had ensured the architects included in their design plans for the space. From the outside, it gave the whole place the appearance of a woodland homestead, something pulled straight out of the pages of a fairy-tale picture book. She usually kept the curtain open, the better to let the light in, but today when she'd gone to begin her work, she'd slammed it shut so the room matched her mood.

Now, she was grateful for the advantage. When she leaned her forehead against the door, she could peer through the small space between it and the curtain, giving her a peek out to where Cole stood.

He was all movie-set made-up, wearing a perfectly tailored lawyer's suit and an expression that told her he was both absolutely certain he needed to be here and also certain he was going to screw it all up.

The whole look—perfectly tousled hair and perfectly tailored jacket paired with constant back and forth pacing and a tormented expression—might have been endearing if Rose's heart hadn't been lodged in her throat, making everything from a normal heartbeat to simple breathing suddenly very difficult.

Based on the complete lack of self-awareness he currently displayed, and the way that he talked to his hands as they punctuated his attempts at speech, he didn't realize she was watching him.

Good. That meant she could really read him. If he didn't think he had an audience, then he wasn't performing. She could see how he truly felt, not whatever act he was trying to put on.

"Yeah. I'm sorry to bother you, but I needed to contact you in our professional capacity. You see, I have a problem."

"Oh, yeah?" she asked, fighting to keep her voice flat and disinterested. "And what problem is that?"

Rose's heart sunk, painful and brutal. He was only here because he'd wanted to ask her a work question? Any grand delusions she might have had about him coming in here, sweeping her off of her feet, and making some epic declaration of love evaporated like snow beneath a heat lamp.

Try as she might, though, and disappointed as she was, she couldn't force her eyes away from him. If he was only here for advice, then this might be the last time she ever saw him in person again. The selfish part of her wanted to commit him to memory, every inch of him, from the broad, warm embrace of his shoulders to the golden light streaming through his hair.

He was beautiful. So beautiful he hurt to look at. It was like looking at a thousand broken promises, a thousand years of love she would never have. At least not with him. It was unfair, she decided, for someone to look so good, to be so wonderful for her, and yet be so far out of her reach.

Finally, his pacing stopped. She watched as he searched for the words in the grass beneath his feet and in the small welcome mat that said, "Knock First" and in the tightly tied laces of his fine leather shoes. When he finally spoke, it wasn't worth the wait.

"Well, I was on set all morning, trying to film a love scene, and I couldn't get it right."

"Sounds like maybe you should try acting. You know, like real actors do."

Over and over again, she reminded herself that their split was for the best, that in the end, they would both be better off for having broken things off. But just because he didn't want to be with her didn't mean that she should suddenly be cruel to him. She knew all of that logically, but her heart and, maybe more importantly, her vocal cords, didn't want to listen to something as remote and bloodless as logic.

"No, that wasn't it. You see, the whole time I was distracted. I was saying these beautiful lines, trying to make this woman fall in love with me on-screen, but every time I opened my mouth to speak…I realized that I wanted to be saying those words to someone else. I wanted to make this grand declaration of love to a real person, for real, this time."

Rose's stomach twisted. The air around her tightened as she processed those words. She didn't dare hope again; she was all out of hope.

"Then maybe you shouldn't have lied to her. Maybe that would have made your big confession of love easier."

"I know. And because of that, I'd like to tell you the truth."

The truth. She wasn't even sure he knew what that word meant. But maybe hearing whatever he had to say would give her closure. Maybe, after this, she could move on from him for good.

"I'm listening."

He drank in a deep breath and began.

"My real name is Ezekiel Andrew Coleman, and I love you."

I love you. It had been implied before, but this was the first time she'd heard him say it in such clear, certain terms.

"I was born in a dustbowl town outside of Oklahoma, and my parents made me sing in the church choir until I ran away from home when I was seventeen. And I love you."

He kept pacing. Her heart was going faster, more and more erratic with every step he took.

"I've always been a romantic at heart, but I convinced myself that I needed to be this untouchable badass if I was ever going to make it in this industry. And I love you."

I love you. Every time she heard it, she felt her walls crumble at her feet.

"Once I got so nervous at a big industry party and stress-ate so much sushi that I passed out on the couch like a racoon who'd gotten locked in a bakery overnight. Oh, and I love you."

He stopped pacing then. She couldn't stop her lips from lifting up at the joke.

"Last week, when I read a romance novel about a couple opening a goat farm, I had a dream that night about you and I doing the same thing. And I love you."

She watched as he, completely oblivious to her presence, pressed the flat of his hand to the door, as if he just wanted to be close to her.

"I haven't always publicly been myself. I've hidden away and pretended and lied. But if there is anything true about me, then it's this. I love you. I think I've loved you from the moment you insulted me at the wine cave. I've loved you every minute more since. And when I was standing on that set today, trying to put our romance lessons to use, I realized that I couldn't go the rest of my life pretending I was in love with someone else. You're right." A small, self-deprecating laugh. He rubbed the back of his neck nervously. "I'm not that good of an actor."

The pause in the conversation indicated that it was her turn to speak. Yet, every time she tried to make the words come out, they all rushed and crammed at the back of her throat. She choked on her own thoughts, her own feelings, as she tried to make sense of them. Apparently, her silence spooked the man outside.

"And I'll leave right now if you never want to see me again. I promise. If you never want to see me again, I understand. I'll leave and never come back. But I didn't think I could spend the rest of my life without having told you the truth."

The truth. That's all she'd ever wanted. Love and the truth. And the man she couldn't stop thinking about was standing just on the other side of this door, offering her both. Finally, her mind and her heart cleared enough for her to get the words out.

"Cole, I thought…I thought I'd been wrong about you. I thought you were just like the person who broke my heart. A lie."

"No. No, absolutely not. You were right all along. I was the one who'd been wrong. And you were right. I was lying. But I wasn't lying to you. I was lying to myself."

"And now?"

She was gripping the curtain with a tight fist, as if it were the only thing keeping her tethered to the ground when her head wanted to go straight up to the clouds.

"Now, I'm being honest. And I'm honestly asking you..." She watched him brace, for the worst and for the best. "Do you feel the same way? Can you feel the same way after how I treated you?"

That was the million-dollar question. Could she? Did she? After a lifetime of hiding and waiting, was she ready to finally have everything she'd ever dreamed of? Real, true, riot-in-the-heart romance? A small smile pulled at her lips, and the first rays of sunshine she'd felt in days crept into her heart.

"I always thought that love was something that would just happen. Like it does in my books. I never thought I would have to chase it. But I don't think that way anymore."

"No?" Cole asked, clear yearning in his voice.

He was feeling it too, that tug between despair and hope. She didn't want to leave him waiting, not for anything in the world.

"No, I think love is something you have to let in. Something you have to accept before it can just 'happen.'"

After a moment of silence, Rose watched as the man she loved approached the door one more time, and knocked. Knock. Knock. Knock.

"And so...will you let me in, Rose?"

Instead of answering his question, she did the only thing she wanted to do in that moment. She threw open the door to her workshop, fell into his arms, and kissed him.

That was better than a promise. After all, he was right. Actions spoke louder than words.

Epilogue

Rose

One Year Later

Today had been a long time coming. When Rose Anderson was a little girl, she wanted to be just like her mother. She had an apron just like hers. She constantly snuck into her closet to try on her makeup and her dresses. She even asked Santa for a calculator, considering that Mama Anderson was the accountant for their family's business and always had her head bent over the finances and figures.

But the trappings of being the family matriarch weren't really what Rose wanted. Sure, hostess aprons and high heels were nice, but the reason she constantly held "family dinners" in her playroom instead of tea parties wasn't because she wanted to look nice.

It was because she wanted to *feel* nice.

There was a certain glow in the Anderson house when the whole family got together, a warmth that radiated through their love for one another. That was the feeling Rose found herself chasing through all of those play-games in her bedroom. *That* was what kept her dreaming, her entire life, of having her own home and her own table for folks to laugh around.

The older she got, the less real that dream felt. On the rare occasions when she let her imagination wander in that direction, the image was hazy, different than it had been when she was little. Instead of a table where she sat beside some man who loved her, she sat alone. Happy, at least, to have the love of her family.

But tonight, the dream finally became a reality. And she realized that sometimes, reality was even *better* than dreams.

There was no way her younger self could have imagined how happy all of her sisters would be with the men they loved. There was no way she could have imagined her father standing to raise a toast to them all, to the Andersons and the Martins and the Rileys and the Barnetts and the McKittricks and the Colemans (who, after some long phone conversations, had finally agreed to meet their son again in person), who all broke bread together at the table that night. Her wildest dreams wouldn't have told her how alive she felt every time she looked at the man sitting beside her, the man who looked at her with all the love she didn't know she would ever get. And they were all here to quietly, warmly, and perfectly celebrate the launch of her first perfume line, a dream she thought she'd never even consider making a reality not so long ago.

The crazy thing about dreams is that you don't realize how much they mean to you until you actually get them. Sure, you imagine that they're going to make you happy—that's why they're dreams, after all—but when you actually have your dream, hold it in your hands…

You realize that the dream is what kept you going for so long. That it was worth fighting for.

And when Rose looked around the table of the house she now shared with Cole—her *own* table with her own family and her own love at her side, all celebrating her biggest accomplishment—she knew that the years of waiting, of wanting, of wondering, were all worth it.

Even that night, when she found herself out on the porch alone, picking at the last of the pie slices Annie and George had brought over as a gift, she stared out into the expanse of their field and remembered the countless nights she'd done this at her old house, the house where she'd grown up. How many lonely nights had she dangled her feet over the edge of the porch, staring up at the stars and wishing for them to show her the way?

Would they answer her now, if she asked?

The house they'd bought together was humble and quaint. Painted white with a slightly sagging front porch that overlooked a front yard planted to the brim with small patches of flowers, it looked like every daydream Rose had ever had. One floor, its façade was mostly made up of old transom windows, the kind you could easily open up in the summer to catch the perfect breeze. Together, they'd installed a swing on the porch, too, where they could spend their evenings eating pie and watching all the black-and-white romances in their movie collection.

The place was a fixer-upper. But they'd known that when they'd bought it. With just enough projects to keep Cole occupied between film shoots and with just enough room for Rose's workshop, where she spent her time away from the florist's shop in town tinkering with her perfumes and designing bouquets for May's upcoming wedding, it had become more than just a house. Like Rose always dreamed, she'd made it into a home with the man she loved. Maybe it had been a bit much, going in together on a piece of property after just a year of dating, but Rose didn't think so.

After all, when you know, you just *know*. And after their one brief moment of doubt so long ago, she'd never again questioned their love. She didn't think she ever would again.

"You look as pensive as you are beautiful," a voice behind her said, as his footsteps traveled to the porch swing where she was currently seated.

Cole. The man who'd made this dream possible. The man who made this dream perfect. The family had left half an hour ago, and he'd let her head out to the porch while he finished up the dishes, offering her a brief respite after the two had spent the whole day on their feet cooking together. But now, as he settled in beside her on the porch swing, she was so glad for his presence, for his warmth, for the smile she heard in his voice. Her head moved to rest on his shoulder. It was cheesy, but his shoulder was one of her favorite places to be. There, she felt safe and secure; all of the questions and doubts seemed to slip into the background whenever she rested there.

"I'm just thinking about dreams. And what we do when we finally get them."

"Oh, I wouldn't know. I haven't gotten my dream yet."

That upward tilt in his tone told her he was approaching a joke. She'd hate to stand in his way. She raised an eyebrow, though she was fully aware that he couldn't see it.

"Is that so?"

"Yep," he said, popping the *p* sound as he spoke. "Do you remember when you came up to my hotel suite, right when we started our little relationship scheme? And I told you that one day, I would move out here to Hillsboro and start a goat farm and you and I would be best friends?"

She did remember that. She also remembered her response had been something along the lines of, "Don't get my hopes up." Oh, if she could go back a year and tell herself what she knew now. She'd tell herself not to be afraid. Not to waste so much time trying to protect her heart.

She'd also, probably, tell herself not to waste so much time *not* kissing Cole.

"I vaguely remember you saying that, yes," she agreed.

"Well, I have the farm. I have my family back. I have my best friend." Cole raised his arm and tucked her beneath it. Immediately, she snuggled in closer to him and rested her hand on his chest, relishing the steady thump, thump of his heartbeat beneath her palm. "The problem is, I don't have the goats yet, do I?"

Rose laughed, but found herself warming up to the idea of a small army of goats. With the residuals from Cole's film career, more projects for him on the horizon, her flower shop still going strong and her perfume business taking off, they could do anything they wanted with this one, precious life of theirs, including founding Hillsboro's first goat and perfume farm.

Still, as happy as she was, the question that had been nettling her since her family left this evening wouldn't leave her alone.

"I just…I wanted this for so long. A life and a love and a home of my own. And now, I have to face the fact that I've had it. I got what I wanted. What do you do when you finally achieve the dream you've been chasing all your life?"

"Well, what are you thinking? You've got to have some idea."

Cole rubbed small circles on her shoulder. She focused on the sensation, allowing it to direct her thoughts and put them all in order until she thought she'd found the right answer.

"Maybe…maybe a dream isn't a one day thing. Maybe you have to wake up, every day, and try to make it come true again."

"I think you're right. And you know what?"

"What?"

Releasing her from the crook of his arm, Cole adjusted their positions on the porch swing so that he could look at her and take her cheeks in his hands.

"Every single day, as long as I'm still part of that dream, I'll be right here with you, helping you get it."

Every word he spoke was a promise, a promise that wrote itself onto her heart.

"Cole?"

"Mm-hm?"

She nestled her cheek closer into his hands, letting her eyes slip closed as she did so. Her lips tingled, waiting for him to capture them with his own.

"You know what I'm dreaming of right now?"

"No, what?"

His smile told her he knew *exactly* what she wanted. But he wanted to hear her say it. Tipping her head closer to him, she let her lips brush against his own.

"A kiss from you."

She loved that she could hear his love for her when he spoke; she loved that no matter what happened, that love traveled between them as easily and freely as air.

"That, we can most certainly arrange."

And as he kissed her beneath the light of the full moon, with the sounds of the wind and the crickets and the porch swing all around them, Rose knew that she would be happy to share this dream with him for the rest of her life.

All she'd ever wanted out of this life was to control her own destiny. This was what she'd chosen, and in her opinion, she'd chosen very, very well.

A Letter from Alys

I want to say a huge thank you for choosing to read *Home at Summer's End*. If you did enjoy it, and want to keep up to date with all my latest releases, just sign up at the following link. Your email address will never be shared and you can unsubscribe at any time.

www.bookouture.com/alys-murray

It is so very hard to say goodbye to Hillsboro, and The Anderson Sisters (plus Annie!). During a global pandemic, a rough patch in my own life, busy work times and stressful personal ones, visiting Hillsboro and The Anderson Sisters has been my respite. My joy! I hope reading this book and the rest of the series brought you as much escape, wonder, and comfort as writing it brought me. I will be forever grateful for the time you spent with me and with my characters, and I hope to see you real soon in Fortune Springs, Colorado, where my next series will be taking place!

I hope you loved *Home at Summer's End* and the rest of this series. If you did, I would be very grateful if you could write a review. I'd love to hear what you think, and it makes such a difference helping new readers to discover one of my books for the first time.

I love hearing from my readers—you can get in touch on my Facebook page, through Twitter, Goodreads or my website.

At the publication of this book, I know we are all in the midst of a difficult time. Thank you for spending some of that time with me, and for trusting me and my characters to help you get through it. Be safe. Be well. Know that you are loved.

All my thanks,
Alys Murray

alysmurrayauthor

@writeralys

@writeralys

18155460.Alys_Murray

Acknowledgments

I can't believe it's time to leave Hillsboro, California behind. When I wrote the first draft of the first book in 2018, I had no idea what lay ahead of me and the journey that would take me here, to the publication of the last book. I wanted to write a series that would help me feel connected to my family in California—my dad, my stepmom, my sisters (Elizabeth, Nia, and Lila), Stella, my grandparents, and my uncle and soon-to-be-aunt. I wanted to wrap up the entire experience of visiting them—the food, the warmth, the love, the connection with nature and the small town where they lived—in a book series, so that no matter where I went, I could carry it around with me. I wanted to share that experience with others. And now, as we turn the page on almost 300,000 words of that experience, I wanted to thank all of the people who made it possible.

First and foremost, I have to thank Emily Gowers, who picked my first book out of the slush pile and decided to take a chance on me. Her friendship, editorial advice, flexibility and encouragement have guided me every step of the way, and made this entire journey not only possible, but one of the best of my life. Kelsie Marsden, who joined our team with *Sweet Pea Summer*, brought so much insight, joy, and enthusiasm to the series, and I am so glad to have had her in my corner. Everyone else at Bookouture—from Peta Nightingale to Sarah Hardy; Radhika Sonagra to Alex Crow; Noelle Holten to Alexandra Holmes; Kim Nash to Leodora Darlington, and everyone in between—has helped me bring this little dream of mine to life, and I am eternally grateful for it. Thank you, with all of my heart.

I also can't finish this series without thanking my family, both the ones listed above, but also Mom, Derek, Maw Maw, Paw Paw, and everyone else who stuck by this series and read it until the very end. Matt Felker (my agent at CAA) is also an angel who listens to all of my pitches—no matter how ridiculous—and all of my wonderful twitter friends (Laurie, Annemarie, Magan, Stacey, Savannah) have helped keep me going during this incredible adventure.

Thank you, Carrie Fisher.

Thank you, to all of the people of Sonoma County, whose perseverance, kindness, and zest for life inspired every page of this series.

And, as always, I can't finish a book (much less an entire series!) without thanking Adam. When we met, I told you my dreams of becoming a writer and braced myself for the inevitable "Oh, so you want to be a waiter?" joke, but it never came. Instead, on that day, and every day since, you have been at my side, supporting me and fighting for me, all so we can make this dream come true. I love you with all of my heart. And yes, to answer your question, all of the romantic heroes in these books are based on you.

Made in the USA
Las Vegas, NV
18 March 2023

69277137R00148